Crazy Imperfect Love

Also from KL Grayson

Touch of Fate series
Where We Belong
Pretty Pink Ribbons
On Solid Ground
Live Without Regret

Dirty Dicks series
Crazy, Sexy Love
Crazy, Hot Love
Crazy, Stupid Love
Crazy, Beautiful Love

Standalone titles
The Truth About Lennon
Black
A Lover's Lament

Short Story Holiday Novella
Naughty or Nice

Short Story Erotica
Double Score

Crazy Imperfect Love

By KL Grayson

A Dirty Dicks/Big Sky Novella

Introduction by Kristen Proby

EVIL EYE
CONCEPTS

CRAZY IMPERFECT LOVE: A Dirty Dicks/Big Sky Novella
By KL Grayson
Copyright 2019
ISBN: 978-1-970077-08-7

Published by Evil Eye Concepts, Incorporated

An Introduction to the Kristen Proby Crossover Collection

Everyone knows there's nothing I love more than a happy ending. It's what I do for a living–I'm in LOVE with love. And what's better than love? More love, of course!

Just imagine, Louis Vuitton and Tiffany, collaborating on the world's most perfect handbag. Jimmy Choo and Louboutin, making shoes just for me. Not loving it enough? What if Hugh Grant in *Notting Hill* was the man to barge into Sandra Bullock's office in *The Proposal?* I think we can all agree that Julia Roberts' character would have had her hands full with Ryan Reynolds.

Now imagine what would happen if one of the characters from my Big Sky Series met up with other characters from some of your favorite authors' series. Well, wonder no more because The Kristen Proby Crossover Collection is here, and I could not be more excited!

Rachel Van Dyken, Laura Kaye, Sawyer Bennett, Monica Murphy, Samantha Young, and K.L. Grayson are all bringing their own beloved characters to play – and find their happy endings – in my world. Can you imagine all the love, laughter and shenanigans in store?

I hope you enjoy the journey between worlds!

Love,
Kristen Proby

The Kristen Proby Crossover Collection features a new novel by Kristen Proby and six by some of her favorite writers:

Kristen Proby – Soaring with Fallon
Sawyer Bennett – Wicked Force
KL Grayson – Crazy Imperfect Love
Laura Kaye – Worth Fighting For
Monica Murphy – Nothing Without You
Rachel Van Dyken – All Stars Fall
Samantha Young – Hold On

Acknowledgments from the Author

First and foremost, I have to thank my husband, Tom. The endless amount of support and encouragement you give me while writing is truly amazing. Thank you for making sure the house stayed clean, the laundry got done, and the kids were fed. Thank you for taking over nighttime duty so that I could stay up late and write. Your love and support is what gets me through the day and I'm so incredibly thankful for you.

A big, big thank you to my dear friend, Kristen Proby and the amazing team at 1001 Dark Nights for inviting me to participate in such a fun project. It has been an honor and so much fun.

To Kristen's loyal readers and fans who took a chance on this crossover novella, THANK YOU! I hope you enjoyed reading Drake and Abby's story as much as I enjoyed writing it!

Sign up for the 1001 Dark Nights Newsletter
and be entered to win a Tiffany Lock necklace.

There's a contest every quarter!

Go to www.1001DarkNights.com to subscribe.

As a bonus, all subscribers can download
FIVE FREE exclusive books!

Prologue

Abby

"What are you doing over here by yourself?" My cousin Hannah plops down beside me and blows a stray curl out of her eyes. Her frilly white gown puffs up around her, pushing into my personal space.

"Resting my feet," I tell her. "These heels are gorgeous, but deadly." Running my hand along her skirt, I grin. "I didn't know a dress could sparkle this much."

"Neither did I. I always thought I'd have a small wedding with a simple gown, surrounded by my closest family and friends."

"You failed miserably."

"I know," she says, smiling from ear to ear.

I do a quick survey of the space. "There's more than a hundred and fifty people here."

"One hundred and eighty-four, to be exact."

"I don't even know that many people. But I guess that's what happens when the local OBGYN marries the beloved police chief."

"I guess." Hannah grabs my Bud Light from the table. "Is this yours?"

I nod, and she hands it to me. Condensation sits thick on the brown bottle. I take a drink and cringe when the warm beer hits my tongue. I take one more swig and hand the bottle back. Hannah laughs and sets it on the table.

"I think this is the first time I've ever seen you drink beer," she notes.

"Figured I'd try something new."

"Speaking of trying something new, have you given any more thought to the job I told you about?"

"I can't move here, Hannah."

She frowns. "Why not? You love it here."

"I do. Montana is great. But I can't just pack up and move."

"Yes, you can. You just said you were looking to try something new."

"Switching up drinks is a lot different than moving halfway across the country."

"Maybe." She shrugs. "But what if it's the sort of change you need? Didn't you tell me last week that your doctor said you need to open yourself up to new experiences, push yourself to try new things?"

I blow out a breath and look at the crowd, hating that she's completely right. Moving is exactly what I need; something to throw me out of my routine, force me to face my fears, and mess up my imperfectly perfect life. Dr. Wallace would probably applaud Hannah for the suggestion. But uprooting my life and moving to a new city isn't a decision that should be made lightly, and it certainly shouldn't be made when I've been drinking.

I turn my gaze back to Hannah. "Are we really going to talk about this at your wedding reception?"

"What are we talking about?" Hannah's friend Grace asks, coming to sit on the other side of me.

I give Hannah a look, and she heeds the warning.

"Taking chances and trying new things," she says, skipping the details of our previous conversation.

Grace nods and motions between me and Hannah. "And which one of you needs to try new things?"

Hannah points to me, Grace nods knowingly, and I roll my eyes.

A waiter walks by with a tray of champagne glasses and Grace snags one. "I tried new things once."

"How did that work out for you?" I ask.

"Pretty damn good," she says, grinning over the rim of her glass.

I narrow my eyes. "What did you do?"

"A stranger," she announces with a proud smile.

Hannah giggles, and I shake my head. "I don't get it."

"What's not to get? She *did* a stranger."

Grace holds up a hand. "Technically, Jacob wasn't the only new thing I did. I also learned how to ski. And he's also not a stranger anymore. He's my husband."

"So, you're telling me I should learn how to ski and bang a complete stranger?"

Grace shakes her head. "I'd go for the stranger and call it a day; skiing is overrated."

"And dangerous, if you're not careful," Hannah adds.

"And she would know, because *careful* is her middle name." Brad's thick hands land on Hannah's shoulders as he bends down to kiss her cheek. "Isn't that right, sweetheart?"

We all look up at Brad's smiling face. His eyes are big, round, and full of love as they shine down at Hannah. If life were a cartoon, he would have hearts floating around his head and Cupid's arrow sticking out of his ass.

Brad is absolutely smitten with my cousin, and I couldn't be happier for them.

I hope someday I find someone to look at me the way he looks at her.

Hannah tilts her head back. "You love that I'm careful."

Brad rewards her with a sweet kiss and reaches for her hand. "It's one of the many things I love about you. Let's dance."

She slips her hand in his. "I'd love to."

"Say goodnight to Abby and Grace, because you probably won't be seeing them again."

"I won't? It's only nine o'clock. The reception doesn't end until midnight."

Brad lowers his lips to Hannah's ear. I can't hear what he says, but it causes Hannah to blush.

"Get a room," I say, playfully nudging the lovebirds.

Hannah is all smiles as she wraps me in a hug. "Thank you for being such a big part of my day. I couldn't have done this without you."

I pull her in close. "I love you."

"I love you too. And I'd love for you to live closer to me," she adds softly.

Rolling my eyes, I pull back. "You don't quit, do you?"

She shakes her head, and I sigh.

"I'll think about it."

That's all the answer she needs. Hannah gives Grace a quick hug before allowing Brad to sweep her onto the dance floor.

Grace finishes her champagne and looks at me. "So, about the str—"

I hold my hand up, stopping her. "I am not going to have a one-night stand."

It's an absolutely terrible idea.

Or maybe the very best.

I cast aside that thought.

Grace shrugs and points across the room. "If you change your mind, start at the bar. I know for a fact that some of Brad's buddies are hanging out there."

"I won't change my mind."

Shaking my head, I watch her walk away. She's crazy for suggesting a one-night stand. It doesn't matter how tempting wild sex with a handsome stranger sounds; it just can't happen.

I'm not the type of girl to throw caution to the wind.

I'm predictable.

Careful.

Boring.

Furrowing my brow, I look at the various women on the dance floor—women of all shapes and sizes being twirled around, laughing and having fun. And what am I doing? I'm sitting here, wishing I was out there. Instead of having fun, I'm mentally planning the next twenty-four hours. A quick look at the clock shows that I have exactly one hour before I need to head back to my room, where I'll pack my bag and go to bed early enough to ensure a solid eight hours of sleep before my flight home in the morning.

Ugh. No wonder I don't have a boyfriend. I'm the oldest twenty-six-year-old in the history of twenty-somethings. Toss in a few cats and some of my grandmother's floral perfume, and I'll be set.

"Come on, Abby!" Hannah hollers, catching my attention. She waves at me from the dance floor where she, Grace, and a few of her other friends are stomping around to some song I only hear at weddings.

Hannah is paying too much attention to me, and she slides to the left instead of the right, knocking into her sister-in-law, Jenna. Brad swoops in like a knight in shining armor, catching her before she topples over, and the girls laugh. I can't help but chuckle along with them, wishing I were an active participant rather than observer.

All too soon, the upbeat music fades to a softer melody, and there goes another opportunity to let loose and have fun. Once again, I've let life pass me by—another missed moment to add to the growing pile. Grace's words slowly seep into my head.

If you change your mind, start at the bar.

My eyes drift across the room to a group of attractive men huddled together on a series of stools.

Damn Grace for putting such a crazy notion into my head. If I can't get out on the dance floor, there's no way I can have a one-night stand. Though the thought does cause a spark of excitement to zip through my veins.

It's a feeling I haven't felt in a long time, and one I'm not ready to let go of.

I grab my clutch, stand up, and move away from the table. Back straight, shoulders square, and chin up, I take a step toward the bar. And then another and another as the electric feeling inside of me grows. And then I stop.

This is insane.

I am insane.

That's the only explanation for what I'm about to do. But I refuse to back down. I refuse to let my anxiety win. Wiping my free hand along the side of my dress, I take two deep breaths—because one is never enough—walk to the bar, and squeeze in where there's an open spot.

The bartender slides a beer to a gentleman two seats down and points to me. "What can I get you, sweetheart?"

"Amaretto and Coke."

"Comin' right up."

The young man steps away as I slide onto an empty stool. Propping a foot on the bottom rung, I relax as best I can and glance to my right. Several men and a few women are grouped together, chatting and laughing.

Before I have a chance to scope what's to my left, a glass lands in front of me. I grab a ten-dollar bill from my clutch, but the bartender waves me off. "Open bar until midnight."

Thank you, Hannah and Brad. I give them a little toast before I take a swig of liquid courage.

"Come here often?" a husky voice says.

I choke, sputtering my drink across the bar, and a large hand lands on my back.

Big mistake. Big, big mistake, because there's no back to this dress, and the feel of this stranger's hand against my skin sparks something inside of me. It isn't just any hand. It's big, strong, warm, and sends a low-level current down to my toes, causing them to curl inside my Jimmy Choos.

Breathe, Abigail, breathe.

That's not the easiest thing because the rich, masculine scent of his cologne is causing me to lose all coherent thought.

"I was trying to make you laugh, not kill you," he says, his voice thick with amusement as he pats my back the way a parent would a small child's.

This time I manage to laugh without spewing alcohol everywhere.

"There it is," he croons, removing his hand from my back and placing it on the bar. "I knew I would love it."

I turn halfway. My eyes lock on his hand first and travel to where the sleeve of his shirt bunches around his elbow. The material is crisp, white, and stretches across his thick forearm.

Oh, sweet baby Jesus, I didn't know forearms could be sexy.

Swallowing, I follow that forearm up to his broad shoulders, and then I go for it—eye contact.

The moment I see his face, my body melts. It's a good thing I'm sitting down, otherwise I'd be a pile of goo on the floor at his feet. He's tall—well over six feet—and quite possibly the most handsome man I've ever seen. His dark hair is messy, giving it that freshly fucked look, and his chiseled jaw looks as smooth as a baby's butt.

Dark brown eyes watch me with a hint of laughter and enough heat that I don't have to guess whether the attraction I'm feeling is mutual. It's clear that he, too, likes what he sees.

My tongue darts out, wetting my bottom lip. His grin is boyish and outlines two rows of straight, white teeth. The longer I stare, the more his smile grows, and when a set of dimples pop up on his cheeks, I know I'm a goner.

Get it together, Abby.

Clearing my throat, I look away and take a sip of my drink. When I'm certain I have my eyes and crazy-ass hormones under control, I meet his gaze.

"I'm sorry, what did you say?"

"I said I knew I'd love it."

"Love what?"

He tilts his head and watches me as if I should already know the answer. "Your laugh."

"How could you know you'd love my laugh?"

"Because you have a mesmerizing smile. It caught my attention from across the room when you were talking to Hannah and Grace."

This makes me sit up straight. "You were watching me?"

"Only for a minute. Why, is that weird?"

For a split second he looks nervous, and I decide I like this look on him just as much as I like the confident one I saw a few seconds ago.

My lips quirk up. "Well, that depends. Are you a serial killer?"

"I can devour an entire box of Lucky Charms in under an hour. Does that count?"

I shake my head and laugh. "That's not what I meant."

He grins and brushes a strand of hair from my face. "I know, but you laughed again, and that's really what I was going for."

Oh my. He's good. "So, you're not a serial killer?"

He shakes his head. "I assure you, I'm not."

"A creeper?"

"Only if you're carrying around a tub of brownies or warm chocolate chip cookies."

"A man after my own heart," I say, pretending to swoon. "Tell me, are you here for Hannah or Brad?"

"Both," he answers.

"Cop?" I ask, curious if he's one of Brad's friends from the force. But he shakes his head.

"I work with Hannah."

"Ah, so you're an OBGYN?"

He shakes his head again. "Actually, I'm not. Why? Do you have a thing against OBGYNs?"

"Not at all. But I don't date doctors."

A look flashes across his face. It's gone as quickly as it appears. "Then it's a good thing I'm not."

"Good to know. You've passed the test." Releasing my glass, I hold my hand out in front of him. "My name is Abigail. My friends call me

Abby."

He places his hand in mine and repeats my name, "Abigail." The way it rolls off his tongue causes my heart to flutter, and I nervously tuck my skirt around my legs. "Delicate and beautiful. It suits you. My name is Drake."

"It's a pleasure to meet you, Drake."

"Trust me, the pleasure is all mine. No woman has ever made me work so hard just to get her name."

"I'm not your typical woman."

He smiles. "Thank God."

After several long seconds, I reluctantly release his hand and reach for my glass—anything to hide what I'm sure is a goofy smile plastered to my face.

"Tell me, Abigail, why a beautiful woman like yourself is sitting at the bar alone."

Twisting my glass against the bar top, I look down. "I'm not sure you want to know the answer."

"Well, now you have to tell me."

I shake my head and take another drink. "You first. What are you doing here?"

"That's easy. I followed you over. Now it's your turn."

"You're good for my ego." Taking a deep breath, I wet my lips. "I can't believe I'm about to tell you this."

Drake holds up a hand. "Wait. Maybe I should be the one interrogating you. Are you a serial killer?"

"No," I laugh, finding myself relaxing. "Well, maybe with Cocoa Puffs."

He sighs. "Good answer. A creeper?"

"Depends. Do you have a bag of Twizzlers?"

"Cherry or strawberry?"

"Strawberry."

"Okay. We can still be friends. I'm ready for you to tell me."

I could make up some stupid excuse and move the conversation along, but there's something about Drake that makes me want to tell him the truth. He's a stranger, for one thing, and I'll likely never see him again. Or maybe it's the feeling I get in the pit of my stomach every time he smiles at me. Either way, I'm going with it.

"Long story short, I need to take more chances in life and try new things. Grace seems to think I should go about that by having a one-night stand with a stranger."

Drake points to himself. "I'm a stranger."

"I know," I say, laughing. "But I came to the bar because I wanted to prove to myself that I could step out of my comfort zone and meet someone new. If I'm being completely honest, I'm not a one-night stand kind of girl."

"Fair enough, although I don't think you should remove it from the table just yet."

"I'm not going to sleep with you."

Drake holds out his hand. "How about a dance then?"

I shake my head. "I don't dance."

"Why not?"

"Because I don't know how."

"There's only one way to learn."

When I don't put my hand in his, Drake reaches for me. I allow him to pull me to my feet, but that's all the farther I'm going.

"I'll step on your toes," I warn.

"That's okay. I have ten."

I laugh for what feels like the hundredth time since he sat down beside me, only this time I find myself leaning toward him. "And I'd prefer you to keep them."

"I'm willing to risk a few."

"I'm not dancing with you."

"What are you afraid of?"

Drake tugs gently on my hand, and I take a deep breath, trying to keep my anxiety in check. Except it doesn't work. My heart rate kicks up a few notches, sending a surge of adrenaline throughout my body.

"N-nothing," I stutter.

"Then dance with me."

Biting my lip, I watch couples glide effortlessly around the room. The thought of being out there with Drake excites and terrifies me.

"What if I'm horrible at it?" I whisper.

His hand tightens on mine. "What if you're not?"

I blink up at him.

What if I'm not?

I'd never thought of it like that before. I always just let fear take over.

"Promise me you won't laugh if I step on your feet, or trip and take us both down?"

With a gentle tug, Drake pulls me to the corner of the room. We're out of the way of the other dancers, but still on the wooden floor.

"I would never laugh at you," he says, wrapping me in his arms. "I've got you, Abigail. Trust me."

Drake holds me close, and I stare hopelessly into his dark brown eyes before my focus dips to his mouth. Those sweet lips have coaxed me into doing something I swore I wouldn't do tonight no matter how much alcohol I had in my system, and I can't help but wonder what else they could convince me to try.

With his arm snug around my back, Drake leans in close. "You're doing wonderfully."

My skin flushes, and in a moment of boldness, I press my body against his. "It's all you."

"Nah. It's us. You fit perfectly in my arms."

His words cause a shiver to race down my spine, and when I find the courage to look up again, I find him watching me intently. We're so close that all I'd have to do is lift up on my toes and our lips would touch. I wonder how soft his would be against mine, or traveling across the base of my neck and down—

"Abigail."

"Yes?" I breathe, dropping my eyes to his chest.

"You can't look at me like that."

"Like what?"

Drake puts a finger under my chin and tilts my face toward his. "Like you want to kiss me as bad as I want to kiss you."

I swallow past the growing lump in my throat—or maybe that's my stomach; I'm really not sure. I do know that if he doesn't kiss me soon, I might kiss him.

"What's stopping you?"

His smile grows as he hauls me in close. Drake is much taller than I am, and I'm forced to lift onto my toes.

"You have no idea what you're getting yourself into," he whispers.

"I could say the same to you."

Chapter 1

One month later

Abby

"How're you feeling this morning, Mrs. Trager?"

The eighty-one-year-old woman grunts and moans as she sits up in bed, but waves me off when I reach out to help her. "I'm good as gold. I don't know why the doc made me stay the night. My third husband had his gall bladder removed and went home the same day."

I open my mouth to respond when the door swings open, bumping into the wall behind it.

"You know exactly why I made you stay overnight," a warm, oddly familiar voice says.

It's the same voice I've dreamed about every night for the last four weeks. The voice that whispered in my ear as its owner brought me to orgasm over and over and over again. I spin around and come face to face with the person who is unknowingly responsible for my move to Cunningham Falls, Montana.

"Drake?"

His piercing brown eyes widen as he steps into the room. He looks as happy to see me as I am him. A slow smile spreads across his face. "Abigail."

"What are you doing here?" I laugh, stepping around the bedside table so I can get a better look at him.

"I could say the same to you."

I point to myself. "I work here."

"So do—"

"Yoo-hoo. Don't forget about me, the patient who is ready to get the hell out of here. What's it gonna take for you to sign those discharge papers, Dr. Merritt?" Mrs. Trager says, cutting him off.

Doctor?

My eyes finally leave Drake's face, and I note the blue surgical scrubs and black stethoscope draped around his neck.

Oh. Hell. No.

This is not happening.

"Excuse us, Mrs. Trager." I walk across the room and stop next to Drake. "Can I speak to you in the hall for a second, please?"

"Sure." He nods before looking at the patient. "I'll be right back, Genevieve, and then we'll get you out of here."

When I step toward the door, Drake follows me. And then he follows me around the corner and down the hall to a small break room, which is thankfully empty. The door shuts quietly behind us, and I whirl around.

"You lied to me."

"No, I didn't."

"Yes. I clearly remember asking if you were a doctor, and you said no."

"No." Drake dips his hands into the pockets of his scrub pants and shakes his head. "You asked if I was an OBGYN, and I'm not. I'm a surgeon."

"That's a technicality." I bristle and clench my jaw. "You lied to me and then slept with me knowing I don't date doctors."

"But we're not dating. *Yet.* And I'm not a doctor. I'm a surgeon."

I point a finger and glare at him. "Don't get cute with me."

That makes him grin. His smile is big and bright and does things to me—delicious things that I most definitely should not be feeling. Especially when I'm mad at him.

"You think I'm cute?" he asks, closing the distance between us.

With each step he takes forward, I take one back, and when my back hits the wall, I growl. "You're not playing fair."

Drake's smile slips, and he steps back from me. "I'm sorry."

"I don't want you to apologize."

"What do you want?"

I want you not to work here.

I want you not to be a doctor.

I want you to kiss me.

The door to the breakroom opens, and a blond nurse I met at the beginning of my shift pokes her head in. She opens her mouth and then closes it.

"Am I interrupting something?"

Drake, the ultimate professional, turns his smile to the young woman. "Not at all. We were discussing a patient. What can I do for you, Farrah?"

"Mrs. Trager keeps hitting her call light. She says if you don't come back in the next thirty seconds, she's yanking her IV out and leaving whether you like it or not."

"Tell her I'm on my way."

Farrah's eyes dart to mine one last time before she slips from the room.

"This conversation is not over," I say, walking past Drake, making sure I don't brush up against him.

"No shit. We have a lot more to talk about."

His firm voice stops me in my tracks. My lips press together, and I plant my hands on my hips. "Like how we need to draw a line in the sand and pretend we haven't seen each other naked?"

Drake's eyes harden, and he has the audacity to look pissed. "There is no line, Abigail. And if there is, we've already crossed it. And I can't pretend I haven't seen you naked, when your body is the only damn thing I've been able to think about since the moment I dropped you off at the airport. Tell me you haven't done the same."

Oh, God, I have done the same. Over and over and over again.

As if he can sense the direction my thoughts are going, his lips curve up into a smirk.

"That's what I thought." Drake steps forward until we're toe to toe and lowers his voice. "All I can think about is how soft your skin is, and the way your body came to life under mine. And your smile and your laugh. *God, I love your laugh.* And don't even get me started on the sweet sounds you made when I—"

"Stop," I beg, trying not to whimper, because that's all I've thought about too—that and how much I want to be with him again. Except that can't happen now because we work together. And to make matters even worse, he's in a position of authority over me. "I'm not sleeping with you again, Dr. Merritt."

"We'll see about that."

* * * *

"Hey." At lunchtime, Hannah slides into a chair across from me in the cafeteria. "How's your day going?"

I swallow the last bite of my sandwich, wad up my napkin, and toss it onto my empty tray. "Pretty good. I'm having a hard time getting used to the electronic medical record system you guys use."

She takes a bite of her apple and nods. "It's tough at first, but once you get the hang of it, you'll love it."

"Mind if I join you, ladies?"

I close my eyes at the sound of Drake's smooth voice. *Was it too much to ask to go the rest of the day without seeing his gorgeous face?* When I hear a chair screech against the floor, I open my eyes in time to see Hannah stand and wrap her arms around Drake's neck.

"Hey, you," she says, kissing his cheek. "I haven't seen you in a while."

There is absolutely no reason for me to be jealous, because Hannah is happily married to Brad, but that doesn't change the tinge of green I feel creeping up inside of me.

"And whose fault is that?" he teases.

Drake's smile is bright enough to light up the room. I stare at him a little too long. Why does he have to be so good-looking?

Thankfully, he takes the empty seat next to Hannah, and as they both sit she says, "Oh, Drake, this my cousin I'm always telling you about, Abby Darwin. I was hoping to introduce you two at the wedding, but you got called in for that emergency splenectomy, and by the time you showed up, I forgot."

Drake's eyes lock on mine, a smile playing at the side of his mouth. "Actually, we did meet at your wedding, but I didn't put two and two together. I had no idea she was your cousin."

"You talked at the wedding? When? Where was I?"

I can tell by the look in Drake's eye that he's remembering exactly what happened the night we met. And the morning after. And just how little talking we actually did.

Swallowing, I look away from him to Hannah. "Toward the end of the night at the reception. We were both sitting at the bar, and I'm pretty sure you were humping Brad on the dance floor."

Hannah grabs a fry and tosses it at me. I duck and stick my tongue out at her.

"We did more than talk," Drake adds.

Is he crazy? I give him a look before turning back toward Hannah. "What he means is we also danced."

The frown on Hannah's face is too cute. "But you don't dance."

Drake unwraps his silverware and lays his napkin on his lap. "Abigail is a great dancer. Although it took some convincing to get her out there."

Hannah lifts a brow. *Abigail?* she mouths, watching me.

I shrug, but I can tell from her side-eye that she's not buying my brush-off.

"Well, it's a good thing you two met, because you'll be seeing Abby a lot."

"I'm looking forward to it." Drake smiles.

Just then, Hannah's pager goes off. She looks down at it, then stands up and grabs her tray. "Gotta go. I've got babies who want to come into this world."

"Are we still on for tomorrow night?" I holler as she walks away.

She spins around but keeps walking. "You, me, wine, and pizza. I wouldn't miss it."

I watch her quick retreat for a moment, and when I turn back to my tray, Drake is watching me. He's got one arm resting on the table and the other draped around the back of the chair Hannah just vacated.

"Stop looking at me like that."

"Like what?" he asks.

"You know what."

Drake laughs and shakes his head. "You're so prickly today. It's sorta turning me on."

My jaw drops open. "Drake," I admonish.

"Abigail," he mocks before sobering his features. "We need to talk about what happened between us."

"There's nothing to talk about. We had se—" I stop myself and look around, making sure no one is too close. Then I lower my voice and continue. "We had sex. Really *great* sex. And then I left."

"Phenomenal sex."

I roll my eyes. "Fine, yes, phenomenal sex. Mind-blowing sex. Better?"

"Much."

"But we agreed it was a one-time thing."

"It doesn't have to be. You live here now. There's no reason we can't see where this thing between us goes."

"There is no *thing* between us. There can't be. Because I'm only here for six weeks."

That causes his smile to disappear. "Six weeks?"

The look on his face makes me wish I could take back my words.

"I'm not here permanently. I took a position with a traveling nurse agency. Hannah knew the hospital was desperate for help, I was looking for a change, and getting placed here was a win-win for both of us."

My night with Drake was so much more than a one-night stand. He renewed my self-confidence. He breathed life into a soul that had been slowly dying over the last several years. He showed me that I can take chances, have fun, and enjoy myself without getting lost in my head. I walked away from him the next morning feeling like a new woman, with a sense of freedom I hadn't felt in…years. I owe him so much, and I would love more than anything to pursue this attraction that smolders between us.

Except we can't.

Drake runs a hand through his already messy brown hair and rests his elbows on the table. "That's not exactly what I was wanting to hear."

I lean back in my seat. "Plus, you're the chief surgeon."

"What does that matter?" He tilts his head, and I see the moment understanding dawns. He sighs and looks down at his hands.

"You're in a position of authority, and the hospital has a strict non-fraternization policy."

"Damn," he huffs, studying his plate as though it holds all the answers. "Now what?"

"I think we do the only thing we can do: agree that our night together was amazing—"

He looks up. "Beyond amazing." He leans toward me and lowers his voice. "The chemistry between us was off the charts. I know you felt it, Abigail."

"God, yes. Of course I did. But my job is important, and so is yours, and neither career is worth a relationship that can't possibly last beyond the next month and a half."

"I don't know if I can work with you every day and not want to touch you."

I clasp my hands together under the table to keep from reaching for him. "Why do you think I was so angry to see you here this morning?"

"I just thought you were upset because I lied. I'm sorry about that, by the way."

"You're forgiven. And I *was* upset about that." I give him a wistful smile. "But I was also upset because I knew it meant we can only be friends."

"Friends," he states.

A thick silence surrounds us. We watch each other, waiting. Eventually, Drake blows out a breath, grabs his tray, and stands up.

"Drake?"

"I don't know if I can be just your friend, Abigail."

Chapter 2

Drake

If something seems too good to be true, it usually is. I've always lived by that rule. That's why I'm not the least bit surprised by the Abigail situation. In today's world, women are ruthless, cold, and after one goddamn thing. Few and far between are the good women—the ones with a genuine heart of gold, sense of humor, and a big, beautiful brain. The second I laid eyes on Abigail, I knew she was a good one. And that was confirmed after spending the night with her.

It killed me to drop her off at the airport the next morning knowing I'd probably never see her again, but I didn't have a choice. Her life was in Texas, and mine was in Montana. After several long kisses goodbye, we decided not to exchange numbers or emails before parting ways. Keep it simple. That's what we decided. But I knew the second I merged back onto the freeway that it had been a huge mistake.

I hate to admit that it took me three weeks to pull my head out of my ass and realize she'd been wearing a bridesmaid's dress that night, and all I had to do was ask Hannah for her information. Which is exactly what I had planned on doing until the woman herself showed up at the hospital—*my hospital*—looking all cute in lavender scrubs with her hair piled on her head in a messy bun and that sweet smile that I can't stop thinking about.

That's the moment I should've known things were too good to be true. A man doesn't get a job he loves, great sex, *and* the girl who gave it to him. That would be way too much to ask for.

I've got the perfect job. I've had the best sex of my life. And now I have to forget the girl.

That last one is proving harder than I thought, and it's only been thirty-six hours since she waltzed back into my life.

I unlock the door to my Tahoe, pull it open, and sink onto the front seat. I drop my head back and groan in pure exhaustion. I'm used to working twelve-hour shifts, sometimes longer. Yet typically when I get off work, I've still got energy to blow at the gym. Today is different. Today I've got nothing but a serious case of blue balls.

All day I waited to see her. I looked for her everywhere—in the cafeteria, the break room, down every hall. It took me four hours to realize she had the day off, and the only reason I got that far was because Hannah told me.

After leaving the lunch room yesterday, I went back to my office and pulled up the company handbook to clarify the non-fraternization policy.

There it was, in big bold letters, telling me what I already knew. Under no circumstances can a supervisor enter into a relationship with a subordinate.

Stupid handbook.

Except it's probably for the best. I need to remember that we live in different states. She might be here right now, but she's eventually going to leave. I may have been able to let her go after our wild night together, but if I get my hands on her again, all bets will be off. There's no way I would be able to walk away a second time.

After starting my car, I let it idle as I look out at the near-empty parking lot. All I can think about is how I'm going home to an equally empty house. Sighing, I press on the brake and move to put my car in drive just as my phone rings. I look down to see Hannah trying to FaceTime me.

Keeping the car in park, I shut it off and accept the call. Her face instantly lights up the screen.

"I need a favor."

"I'm all out of favors."

"No." She pouts. "Why are you all out of favors?"

"Because it's been a long day. I had three emergency

appendectomies, one of which was a three year old. Dr. Fullerton lost a patient during a routine procedure. And to top it off, I ended up removing shards of glass from the head of an eighty-three-year-old woman who pressed the gas instead of the brake and rammed through the front of a building."

Hannah's eyes are wide as she watches me. "Wow. You did have a long day. If it makes you feel better, I delivered six babies. Four vaginally and two via emergency C-section. One of the babies had a sixth toe I had to remove, which shouldn't have been a big deal, but the parents freaked out. Another baby suffered from meconium aspiration, and another was born with an unexpected birth defect."

"Fine. You win. I don't know how you work with babies. They're completely unpredictable. And don't you have the means to detect birth defects?"

"Mom opted against the testing during her prenatal care."

"Damn."

"Now will you do me a favor?" She waggles her eyebrows. "It's one I think you might like."

"I'm listening."

"I need you to go to Abby's and help her put a few things together."

"Aren't you supposed to go help her? What happened to pizza, wine, and girl time?"

"I've got a mother laboring, and I can't leave."

It's on the tip of my tongue to tell her no, but the thought of seeing Abigail after such a long, shitty day sounds pretty damn good. I'm a sucker for funny, beautiful women.

"Fine. Give me her address."

"I knew you liked her," Hannah says, punching the air. I narrow my eyes, and she lowers her fist. "I—I mean, I knew you'd say yes. Because you're a good guy. The best. And I love you."

"Love you too. Goodbye, Hannah."

"Don't forget the pizza," she adds before I can end the session.

"Pizza. Got it."

"She likes St. Louis style with pepperoni and bacon."

"Where the hell am I going to find St. Louis-style pizza? We're in Montana."

"That little pizza joint downtown makes it. But you have to request it as a special order. It's not on their menu."

"Okay," I say. "St. Louis style, pepperoni and bacon."

Hannah nods. "Tell her I'm sorry I couldn't make it."

"Shouldn't you call her and tell her you can't make it? And maybe mention that I'm coming in your place? You know, in case she wants to decline."

"But that would ruin the surprise."

"I'm not sure a surprise is what either of us needs right now."

"That's where you're wrong. Trust me on this, okay? And then thank me later. Gotta go."

She ends the call before I have a chance to respond. Ten minutes later I'm pulling up to Alfonzo's Pizzeria, and twenty minutes after that I'm heading toward the address Hannah texted me.

I'm about a mile away when the neon lights of a local convenience store catch my attention. In a split-second decision, I pull the wheel to the right and make another stop—one I hope will put a giant smile on Abigail's face.

Chapter 3

Abby

There's a soft knock at the door, and I look at the clock. Hannah and I didn't set an exact time, but she said she'd come by after her shift, which ended over an hour ago. Dropping the screwdriver to the floor, I walk across the small apartment and swing open the front door.

"What took you so lo...?" I say, my words trailing off when I see Drake standing in my doorway instead of Hannah. "Where's Hannah?"

"She said to tell you she's sorry, but she had to work late."

"So, she sent you instead?" *Thank you, Hannah.*

Drake holds up a pizza and nods. "I come with provisions. Are you going to invite me in?"

I cross my arms over my chest. "That depends," I say. "What kind of pizza did you bring?"

"Only the best kind. Pepperoni and bacon."

I snatch the box from his hands and all but sprint to the kitchen. I hear the front door shut behind me, and I assume Drake has followed, but I don't turn around to find out. I flip open the cardboard box, and my stomach growls at the sight in front of me.

Drake laughs. "Hungry?"

"Starving. I haven't eaten since breakfast."

He looks at his watch and furrows his brow. "It's almost eight-thirty at night."

"I'm aware," I say, placing a hand over my stomach when it growls again.

Drake pushes the pizza toward me. "What are you waiting for? Dig in."

Forgoing a plate, I pull a square from the box. The gooey cheese explodes in my mouth, and I moan. "This is amazing."

I take another bite, this time closing my eyes, but when Drake clears his throat, they pop back open.

My cheeks heat as I realize how I must've sounded. "Sorry," I mumble, swallowing my bite of food.

"I never thought I'd get turned on by watching a woman eat."

"You're turned on right now?"

"Incredibly." Drake takes a step forward. "You've got a little something…" He raises his hand, inches away from my face, and for a moment I think he's going to use the pad of his thumb to wipe away whatever he sees.

My heart beats faster, but he lowers his hand and takes a step back. Stupid, hopeful heart.

Instead, he points to the side of my mouth. "You have some sauce."

"Oh." My tongue darts out, licking it away. "Thank you. Aren't you going to have a piece?"

"If you don't mind."

"No, please, have as much as you want. Want something to drink?"

"What've you got?"

"Water, sweet tea, and milk."

"I'll have a water."

I take two waters from the refrigerator. When I nudge the door shut with my hip, I notice it doesn't close as fluidly as my fridge at home. After I give Drake his bottle of water, I press my hand to the front of the fridge, give it a little push to make sure it's sealed, and then run my fingers along the crack down the middle to make sure both doors are shut. At home, if one of the doors isn't completely closed, they'll be uneven when I run my hand down it.

"Is something wrong with your fridge?"

I spin around to find Drake watching me curiously. "Oh…" I shake my head. "No. I was just… The door sticks a little, and I was making sure it was shut."

Because if it isn't, then all of the food I just bought will spoil, and I'll have to throw it out and make another trip to the grocery store, not to mention the money that would be wasted.

And just like that, the familiar uneasiness I've grown accustomed to sets in. It settles like a lead weight in my belly, begging me to keep checking the door until the restless feeling subsides.

Come on, Abby, don't do this. Not today. Not in front of Drake.

I take a deep breath and press my hand to the door one last time.

This is the last time I'm going to check the door. It's shut. The door is shut, and I'm being ridiculous.

"Want me to take a look at it? Maybe the hinges need to be loosened."

"No, it's okay. I'm sure it's fine."

Drake shrugs, grabs a piece of pizza, and takes a bite. As my stomach settles and the weight slowly dissipates, I allow myself a second to give him a onceover. He wears a set of surgical scrubs that look identical to the ones he was in yesterday morning, only these are a little tighter around the chest, making me wonder if he works out. Who am I kidding? Drake is probably one of those guys who gets an hour of cardio in and a shower before I even consider rolling out of bed.

I raise my eyes to Drake's when he moans, hoping I wasn't staring too much.

"This is great," he says, lifting his pizza. "I've never had St. Louis style before."

"It's the Provel cheese—makes all the difference. Did you come straight here from work?"

He nods, finishes off his square, and goes in for seconds.

"You didn't have to do that."

"I wanted to."

I can't remember the last time a man did something this nice for me. The last memory that comes to mind was when my father made it to one of my dance recitals. Afterward he presented me with a bouquet of flowers before darting back to work. It was the only recital he made it to in the five years I danced, and to this day I'd be surprised if he remembered.

"Thank you."

Drake's hand stops halfway to his mouth. "You're welcome."

We eat the rest of the pizza in silence, enjoying our meal, and when

I toss the empty box in the trashcan, Drake perks up.

"I have something for you," he says, slipping out the front door.

A few seconds later, he returns with his hands behind his back.

"What do you have?"

"Dessert." Drake lifts his hands, revealing a bag of strawberry Twizzlers.

"You remembered."

He hands me the bag. I pull it open, grab a Twizzler for myself, take a bite, and hand one to Drake. "And they're strawberry."

"That's your favorite."

"It is. I can't believe you remember."

"I haven't forgotten a single thing from that night."

I rip off another bite and chew it slowly, wondering what I'm supposed to say to that. All that comes out is the truth. "Neither have I."

Drake's eyes fall to my mouth. For a moment, I wonder if he's going to kiss me. And if he does, there's no way I'll be able to push him away. He blinks several times and then shoves his hands in his pockets and spins around.

"Hannah said you need help putting something together?"

"Oh, uh, yeah. Follow me."

* * * *

Drake

It only takes twenty minutes to put Abigail's bedframe together, so I take my assistance a step further and make the bed using a stack of sheets and comforter I find sitting in the corner. When I'm done, I walk through the small apartment and find her rearranging the cabinets in the kitchen.

"That bed is huge. It barely fits in the room."

Abigail turns around, hops up on the counter, and pulls the band from her hair. Black waves tumble over her shoulders, and my mind drifts back, remembering what it felt like to have the tips of her hair tickle my thighs as she rode my cock. I'm immediately lost in the memory of her nails digging into my chest, sweet moans of whispered pleasure, and the way her body felt wrapped around mine.

"Drake?"

"Yeah?" I say, snapping out of it.

"Did you hear what I said?"

"Not a word. Sorry, I spaced out."

Abigail smiles as she twists her silky locks on top of her head. "I was telling you about how weird it was moving into a furnished apartment."

"Is it part of your contract with the agency?"

"Yes. They pay for the housing and travel, and I get a meal stipend. I just wish they would've told me I'd have to put all the furniture together. I didn't exactly have the tools to do it."

"I had all the tools I needed back there."

"That's because I made an emergency trip to the hardware store and told the worker I needed all the equipment to put together a bed frame and coffee table. Tools were not among Hannah and Brad's wedding gifts."

"You should've called me. I would've brought the tools over. You didn't have to go buy them."

"I would've, except I don't have your number." Abigail looks down and adds, "Plus, I wasn't sure where we stood after yesterday."

I hate that Abigail is here, in my hometown, mere feet away from me, and I can't be with her. I can't touch her or hold her; all I can do is look at her. But what I hate even more is that she thought for a second she couldn't reach out to me.

I tip my chin and nod toward her phone sitting on the counter. "Toss me your phone."

She flips it across the room, and I catch it against my chest. I pull up her contacts, add my number, and toss it back.

"There. Now you can call me anytime."

Abigail's eyes are wide as she looks down at her cell, and I swear I see them well up with tears.

"Abigail?" I take a step forward, but when she looks up, I stop. Because if I go to her, I'll touch her, and that's something I can't allow myself to do. "I'm sorry about what I said in the cafeteria…about not being sure if we can be friends."

She smiles tremulously and shrugs a shoulder. "It's okay. I understand."

"No, it's not okay. I was just angry and a little bitter because I really like you. But if you're up for it, I'd love for us to try to be friends."

"I'd like that a lot."

There isn't much more to say, and I'm not really in the mood to talk, so I motion toward the bedroom. "I'm going to go grab the screw gun, and then I'll put this coffee table together."

I feel her eyes on me as I walk down the hall. When I enter the bedroom, I stand for several long seconds, take more than a few deep breaths, and then head back into the living room. Without looking in Abigail's direction, I park my ass on the floor and go to work putting the legs on her coffee table.

"Drake?"

"Yeah?" I ask, pushing the final screw in.

"I really like you too," she says softly.

My head snaps up, but rather than looking at me, Abigail is concentrating hard on organizing her cabinets. I know she can feel me watching her; it's in the way her chest rises and falls just a little bit faster and the tremor in her hand. But not once does she stop and look my way. She stays focused on the task at hand, meticulously lining up all of the cups by size.

The tallest glasses in the back taper to the shortest in the front. None of them are stacked on top of each other, and I notice her spice cabinet—which is open—situated much the same way. When she moves to the plates, I can't help but laugh.

She would have a heyday if she saw my kitchen.

Chapter 4

Abby

"Hey, thank you again for your help the other night," I call.

It's been three days since I've seen Drake, and I'm more than a little surprised when he bustles by me down the hospital hallway without stopping.

"Anytime."

His brows are pulled tight, and the easygoing smile I'm used to seeing is absent.

"Is everything okay?"

He shakes his head and keeps walking. I have to take two steps for every one of his just to keep up.

"What's wrong?"

"Two surgical techs called in sick. Darlene is in the bathroom throwing up, and I've got to be in surgery—" He looks at his watch. "—ten minutes ago, and I don't have a scrub nurse."

"I can help."

That makes him stop.

"I worked as a scrub nurse at my last job. I'd be more than happy to step in if you can find someone to cover my assignment on the floor."

"Done." Drake leaves me in the hall and walks to the nurse's station with purpose.

He stops in front of Cindy, the charge nurse. They exchange a few words, which I'm unable to hear, and then I see her nod and stand up.

When Drake walks back by, he says, "Go give report on your patients and meet me in the OR."

Ten minutes later, I'm scrubbed in and standing beside Drake and his team in surgical suite #2.

Lucy, the other RN in the room, was fine taking over the circulating nurse responsibilities for this operation. We thought it would be best since she knows the layout of the room. I've scrubbed in for enough surgeries that I can comfortably assist Drake during this procedure. And then there's Barbara, who's acting as RN first assistant and will spend the majority of the surgery monitoring the patient for signs of distress.

"Abigail, this is Dr. Connor," Drake says, nodding toward the man sitting at the head of the patient's bed. "He's the anesthesiologist with us today. Bruce, this is Abigail. She'll be working on the med-surg floor for the next several weeks."

"Welcome," he says, offering me a warm smile.

Drake preps the patient and nods to Lucy. A second later, rock music filters through the speakers, and Drake holds out his hand.

"Scalpel."

"I didn't peg you for a Led Zeppelin fan," I say, handing him the instrument.

Every surgeon is different. Some blare the music—songs and artists you'd never expect—while others like silence. I prefer it like this, just enough music to drown out the sounds of surgery, but not so loud that you can't carry on a conversation.

Dr. Connor chuckles behind his mask as Drake concentrates on the patient. "None of us did. I swear this kid grew up in the wrong generation."

"Wait until you hear him belt out the lyrics to Black Sabbath," Barbara says.

If Drake's face weren't covered by the mask, I'm sure I'd see him smile—his eyes crinkle above it.

"Only during surgery and when I hike."

"You hike?" I don't know why I'm surprised. This is Montana, after all.

He nods, and Dr. Connor continues to carry the conversation. "He does it all. Snow skiing, hiking, snowboarding, mountain biking—"

"Snowshoeing," Drake adds.

"If it's an outdoor activity, he's doing it. What about you, Abigail? Are you the outdoorsy type?"

"Please, call me Abby. And I'd like to say yes, but honestly, I've spent the last five years consumed with college and starting my career. So I haven't gotten to do much more than study and sleep."

"Where are you from?" Barbara asks, monitoring one of the many machines in the room.

"Kansas, but I've lived in Heaven, Texas, most of my life."

"I've been there once. It's beautiful and hot. How are you handling the temperatures here?"

"Not too bad. I had to stock up on winter clothes, but it's honestly not as cold as I expected."

"You came in at the tail end of winter, and it's been mild for us this year."

"I know, I was hoping there would still be snow on the ground. I've only seen snow once in my life, and it was only half an inch."

Everyone laughs.

"That isn't snow," Lucy says. "We're supposed to have a cold front come through next week. If you're lucky, you might get to see what real snow looks like."

"I'll keep my fingers crossed."

Our conversation dies off, and we work silently side by side as Drake repairs the inguinal hernia. I follow along with him, anticipating his needs and handing him various instruments before he has a chance to ask for them.

As Drake finishes up with the actual surgery, he glances at me. "You're pretty good at this."

"Thanks."

"We're always looking for good nurses in the OR, if you ever consider making your stay here permanent."

Our eyes connect over the rims of our masks, and I'd give anything to know what he's thinking. But Drake doesn't give me much time to analyze.

"Let's get things cleaned up, and I'll close the patient."

There's a flurry of activity as everyone assumes their roles, and I begin counting the instruments, sponges, and other tools Drake has used.

When the instruments are set aside and I've informed Drake of the count, I turn back to count the sponges again. You can never be too careful when it comes to the sponges. Although it's never happened on my watch, I've heard about patients being stitched shut with sponges still inside of them. That obviously leads to complications.

One. Two. Three. Four. Five. Six. Seven. Eight. Nine. Ten. Eleven.

One. Two. Three. Four. Five. Six. Seven. Eight. Nine. Ten. Eleven.

One. Two. Three. Four. Five. Six. Seven. Eight. Nine. Ten. Eleven.

I stack them up and then separate each one, laying them out on the tray as I count them again.

One. Two. Three. Four. Five. Six. Seven. Eight. Nine. Ten. Eleven.

"Abigail?"

I glance up at Drake. "Yeah?"

"Are there eleven? That's how many I used."

"Um, yeah…I was just making sure."

He looks at me for a long moment and then nods. "It's better to be sure. Go ahead; count them again."

I almost breathe a sigh of relief. I've had doctors scold me after surgery for taking too long to count the sponges and instruments. In reality, they should be thanking me for possibly saving them from a horrible lawsuit that could cost them their license and hundreds of thousands of dollars—and maybe even a patient's life.

One. Two. Three. Four. Five. Six. Seven. Eight. Nine. Ten. Eleven.

This time when I count them, I touch each sponge individually, cataloging it in my head.

Drake sits patiently while I go through my ritual, seemingly unfazed by my odd behavior. Generally, when someone happens to see me during a bout of counting, I get more anxious. But it's not like that with Drake.

And it wasn't like that the other night when he caught me checking the refrigerator.

He has a soothing presence. With him, I feel calm.

Accepted.

When I'm confident that all of the sponges are accounted for, and there's not a lick of unease in my veins, I report the number to Drake again.

His smile once again reaches his eyes. "Thank you, Abigail. Great job, everyone. Let's get this patient into recovery."

Lucy and Barbara wheel the patient out. Dr. Connor is not far behind them, and when the room is empty, Drake peels his gloves off, lowers the mask from his face, and looks at his watch.

"My shift is over in twenty minutes. Want to grab a bite to eat?"

My stomach flutters. The angels sing from above. And then the annoying voice in my head reminds me—*you can't be together.*

Stupid voice.

But since when does having dinner mean we're *together?* Men and women have dinner all the time without bedding each other at the end of the night. Drake and I are perfectly capable of sharing a nice meal without allowing it to lead into dangerous territory.

"I'd love to."

His smile is positively brilliant. "I know a great place. If it's okay with you, I'll follow you home and you can jump in with me."

"Perfect."

I'm not dating him. I'm not sleeping with him. This is completely innocent. Drake might be my supervisor, but he's also best friends with my cousin Hannah, who happens to be *my* best friend, so basically that makes Drake and me best friends. And best friends hang out all the time. Plus, we're professionals.

Professionals and friends. Nothing more, nothing less. That's what I keep telling myself as he follows me home, and again as I jump out of my car and climb into his.

Friends.

We're just friends.

Chapter 5

Drake

"I could've followed you," Abigail says, reaching over her shoulder to buckle up.

"You could've, but then I wouldn't have gotten to spend the extra time with you."

Her head whips around in surprise. Her jet black hair makes her icy blue eyes pop. I could get lost in them, drown in them without once thinking to come up for air. They're hypnotizing, and if she'd let me, I'd stare at them forever.

"You look beautiful, Miss Darwin," I whisper, glancing at her.

She looks good sitting in my truck, like she's meant to be here with me.

"This ole thing?" she quips, running a hand down the front of her navy blue scrubs. She bites her lip and nods toward me. "You don't look too bad yourself, Dr. Merritt."

Something about the way she says my name doesn't sit right with me. Tonight, I don't want to be her supervisor—or even her coworker.

"Tonight I'm just Drake. Is that okay?" I turn my attention back to the road.

"You got it, *Just Drake.*"

Fuck me, she's adorable. "Smartass."

Abigail grins. "Where are you taking us?"

"You'll see."

"I hope it's not fancy," she says, looking at my scrubs. "We look hot and all, but I'm not sure scrubs qualify as proper attire for most restaurants."

"It's not fancy."

"Ah, so you're taking me to a hole in the wall?"

I laugh. "Would you stop asking questions and just relax? It's a surprise, and I promise you're going to love it."

"That's a big promise, *Just Drake*. I don't fall in love easily."

You loved my lips on the base of your neck and the feel of my body between your legs. And if you gave us a chance, you could probably fall in love with me.

Whoa. Where the hell did that come from?

Love?

No fucking way.

Swallowing hard, I glance at Abigail. "I guess you'll just have to trust me."

"I think I can do that." With a sweet smile, she relaxes against the leather seat. "Let the relaxing and trusting commence."

We don't have far to go. I make the three-mile drive to the outskirts of town and then another mile past the on-ramp to the interstate. When I pull into a desolate parking lot and the pink neon lights come into view, Abigail perks up.

"Welcome to Abby's," I announce, putting my car into park. "Home of the best burger in Montana."

"Shut the front door!" Abigail laughs. She hops from my truck and walks toward the front of the diner with a look of awe on her face.

I climb out and follow behind. She spins around and pins me with her signature smile, the one that reaches the deepest parts of my heart.

The one I'm falling for.

"This is crazy!"

"Wait until you taste the food. It's delicious." I grab her hand and lead her toward the front door.

"I don't believe this. I've been to Cunningham Falls twice to visit Hannah, and she never mentioned this place."

"She probably doesn't know about it. Abby's is sort of a hometown gem. Unless you were born and raised here, or know someone who was, you've likely never heard of it. Most people don't drive out this way."

"It is sort of an odd spot for a diner," she says, looking around.

"It's the middle of nowhere."

A bell chimes when I open the front door. "There's a sweet story about the location."

"Tell me everything," she says, walking in ahead of me.

I nod to the only waitress in the joint and follow Abigail to a booth in the corner.

"This place is wonderful," she says.

My eyes follow hers around the room, seeing everything for the first time. The floor is black and white checkered. The booths are metallic and red. Old Coca Cola décor lines the walls, and then there's the very best piece, the jukebox, which is currently playing Dion & The Belmonts' "A Teenager in Love," which is fitting for the story of how this diner came to life.

"The story goes a little somethin' like this..." I begin. "John Truman married his childhood sweetheart, Abby Tallman. The first house they lived in as a married couple sat right here—"

"Like, right here, right here?"

"Right here, right here," I confirm. "In this exact spot. They spent fifteen years in the house, where they had four children. John was a carpenter, and Abby was a teacher."

"I love her already. I bet she was wonderful."

"Abby loved to cook and bake, and it was her dream to open her own restaurant. She never fulfilled that dream because one evening the house caught fire. John was at work when it happened, and everyone made it out except Abby. She died saving her children's lives."

Abigail sucks in a breath and covers her mouth with her hands.

"John was devastated. Abby was the love of his life. He never remarried, and he finished raising their children down the road in an old farmhouse. When his kids grew up and moved away, he spent his life's savings to build this diner."

A tear rolls down Abigail's cheek. "He fulfilled her dream for her. That's the worst and best story I've ever heard."

I nod. "It's a tragic story, but also very beautiful. There's a picture of Abby on the wall in the hallway."

"What about John? Is he still alive?"

"Oh yeah, he's still kickin'. He's got a bad hip, so he isn't here as much as he'd like to be, but her memory lives on, and that's all he really wanted."

"If I die tomorrow, will you open a turtle sanctuary in my name?"

I smile, unsure if she's joking or not. "You're serious?"

Abigail nods. "Very much. I've always loved turtles and tortoises. When I was a little girl, I swore I was going to rescue turtles for a living."

"Is that even a thing?"

"Sure. People rescue dogs and cats, right? Who rescues the turtles?"

"Well, aren't most turtles wild?"

"Don't ruin this for me, Drake."

"Sorry." I chuckle and hold up my hands. "Keep going."

"My eight-year-old self wanted nothing more than to rescue turtles in need. My parents used to laugh at me. Dad always said I'd better get a good job because it was going to be an expensive hobby."

"If something happens to you, I solemnly swear to open a turtle sanctuary," I say, using my finger to make a cross over my heart.

"Thank you. And if you die tomorrow, what should I do for you?"

I think back to my childhood, and nothing stands out. For as long as I can remember, I've wanted to be a doctor. There were no wild dreams or crazy hopes of rescuing animals or having my own restaurant. I always wanted to save lives.

"You can build a turtle sanctuary."

Abigail tilts her head to the side. "But that's my dream."

"I know. And if I die tomorrow, you can honor me by fulfilling your dream."

She watches me for a long moment and then reaches across the table and covers my hand with hers. "You're one of the good ones, Drake Merritt."

I open my mouth to tell her it's not just me, but her too, and how wonderful we could be together, but I don't get the chance.

"Hey, Dr. Merritt," Jess says, startling Abigail.

She quickly pulls her hand from mine and shoves it in her lap under the table.

Jess doesn't seem to notice, or she doesn't particularly care. She pulls a notepad from her pocket and a pencil from behind her ear. "I haven't seen you in a while."

"Work has been keeping me busy. Jess, this is my friend Abigail. Abigail, this is Jess, one of John's granddaughters."

Abigail smiles politely. "It's a pleasure to meet you."

"You too," Jess says, chomping on her gum. "You guys ready to order?"

"Oh, uh…" Abigail looks around. "We never got menus."

Jess frowns, and I intercede. "Do you trust me?"

Abigail looks from me to Jess and back to me. "Uh…yes?"

"Come on, you can do better than that. Do you trust me?"

"Yes!" she chants with the enthusiasm of a high school cheerleader. "I trust you."

I look at Jess to order our meals, but I can't even concentrate because now all I can think about is Abigail in a tiny cheerleading outfit. And then it's visions of bending her over, wrapping her ponytail around my hand, flipping that skirt up, and burying myself in her tight heat. She'd chant my name the same way—

A voice clears.

I blink and look up to find Jess staring at me. "We'll both have a number six."

"What's a number six?" Abigail asks when Jess walks away.

"You'll have to wait and see."

Chapter 6

Abby

"That was the best bacon cheeseburger I've ever had. When you told me to trust you, I thought you were going to order something crazy."

"I wasn't sure if you were the type to order a salad, and I really wanted you to try the burger because it is the best."

Scrunching my nose, I shake my head. "I'm addicted to all things greasy, fatty, and loaded with way too much sugar."

"I'll keep that in mind."

Just then the bell on the front door chimes and a group of people walk in. They wave at Drake as they take their seats on the opposite side of the room.

"Is it okay that we're here together?" I ask, leaning toward the table.

"Of course. That's Janice Ditmer, her oldest son, Jack, and his wife, Carly. Trust me, they don't care who I'm here with—not that it's any of their business."

"I know, but I don't want you to get in trouble for being here with me. What if someone from the hospital sees us here together?"

"We're not doing anything wrong, Abigail. We're having dinner."

"If you're sure."

"I'm positive. Now, what should we have for dessert?"

My eyes widen. "How can you possibly be hungry for dessert?"

"How can you not?" he admonishes.

I snag the dessert menu from the table and open it up as the bell chimes again. This time an older couple walks in, and when the husband sees Drake, he shuffles his way toward us.

"How ya doin', Dr. Merritt?"

Drake stands and greets the man and his wife with a warm smile. "I'm well, thank you for asking. How are you doing?"

"A lot better now that those damn hemorrhoids are gone. You perform the best damn hemorrhoidectomy this side of the mountains." The old man chuckles, his round belly bouncing.

I nearly spew my drink across the table. I'm a nurse, so I get talking about gross stuff, even while I eat, but why on Earth would a patient want to talk about hemorrhoids in the middle of a restaurant?

Drake is unfazed. "Good to hear."

"Now I just need to get the damn bunions taken care of, and I'll be a new man."

"You know how to find me."

"That I do." The gentleman notices me for the first time and smiles. "Who's this beautiful woman?"

"This is my friend, Abigail. You remember Dr. Malone—Dr. Hull now—don't you?"

The old man looks a little confused, but his wife smiles brightly. "Yes, I know Hannah. She's my gynecologist. In fact, I just saw her last week for a raging yeast infection."

That makes Drake flinch. "Well, hopefully she got that all fixed up for you. Anyway, Abigail is her cousin."

"It's so nice to meet you, dear," the woman says. "If you see Hannah, tell her Gwen's itch is gone. She'll know exactly who you're talking about."

Oh boy. I smile and nod, and the woman turns to her husband. "We should probably order. It's getting late."

The older man shakes Drake's hand once more and tips his hat in my direction. "Good seeing you again, Dr. Merritt. Sorry if we interrupted your meal."

"No worries, Mr. Gardner. We were finished anyway. Enjoy your meal and drive home safely."

We watch the couple shuffle across the diner and take a seat in the corner.

"I bet that happens to you a lot."

"It's a small town. I know almost everyone, and if they've had surgery, I was probably the one who performed it."

"Well, that was really nice of you."

"What was?"

"Talking to Mr. Gardner."

Drake shrugs as if it's not a big deal, except it is.

"You're off the clock, and you took time out of your evening to talk to them, even if it was just for a couple of minutes."

"Any doctor would've done the same."

I shake my head adamantly. "That's not true. My parents would've brushed them off and rushed them along."

Drake's eyes narrow. "Your parents are doctors? You've never mentioned that. What kind of practice are they in?"

"My father is a cardiovascular surgeon, and my mother is an oncologist."

"Wow."

"Yup. They are very smart and *very* busy. Mom owns her own cancer treatment center, and Dad teaches cardiovascular surgery at the local university."

"Impressive."

I shrug. "If you call being married to your job impressive, then yes."

"You're not impressed."

"Of course I am. I'm proud of their successes. I love my parents dearly. They gave me many opportunities in life that others don't get."

"But those opportunities came with a price?" he guesses.

"A hefty price. I never saw them. They were gone when I got up, and I was asleep by the time they got home. They missed recitals and Christmas concerts and every single soccer game I ever played. I was raised by a revolving door of nannies."

Drake's face falls. "That must've been hard on you."

"It is what it is."

"I'm surprised they didn't push you to follow in their footsteps."

"Oh, trust me, they tried. But I saw how their careers dictated their lives—I was a product of it—and I swore I'd never subject myself or my family to that lifestyle."

Although for you, I think I would try.

"That's why you don't date doctors."

I point a finger at him. "Bingo."

"I won't lie and say I don't love my job, because I do. I think most doctors love their job—they have a passion for it—which is why it's so hard for them to step away sometimes. But we're not all like your parents."

I gasp. "You mean you know how to relax and have fun?"

We both laugh at my lack of acting skills. "Yes, I know how to have fun."

Laughter from another table catches my attention. I turn to look at small group of people who have been here for almost as long as we have. They too said hi to Drake when they walked in, which is why I've been careful not to touch him as openly as I did when we got here, but it's hard when I'm having such a good time.

"You're thinking awfully hard over there. What's on your mind?"

"Nothing." I shake my head. "I was just thinking about how much fun this has been. I can't remember the last time I spent time with someone who wasn't a classmate and talked about something other than school."

"I've had a wonderful time too."

I study my empty plate before looking up and catching Drake's eye. "I can't help but wonder how differently tonight would've gone if we weren't Abby and Drake."

"What do you mean?"

"This might sound silly, but I wish we could be two different people. Just for one night."

"Two strangers?"

"Yes. Like how we were when we first met, before you became my superior. Only this time, maybe we're two strangers who meet at a restaurant. I just finished a wonderful meal, and I'm perusing the dessert menu when a guy from across the room catches my attention."

"What's your name?" Drake asks, playing along with my silly game.

"Bethany."

Drake slides from the booth and walks across the restaurant. I look around and laugh, wondering what in the world he's up to when he stops to talk to Jess. When he comes back, he stands in front of me and holds out his hand.

"Excuse me, but I couldn't help but notice you from across the room. Are you here alone?"

I can't believe we're doing this. "I am…" I hesitate, and when Drake stays in character, I continue. "But I'd love some company."

He smiles and holds out his hand. "My name is Tom."

"Bethany," I say, shaking his hand.

Drake…er, Tom slides onto the empty seat. "Was your meal good?"

"Wonderful. It was my first time eating here. A friend recommended it."

"Must be some friend. Great taste if he recommended a place like this."

"He is a wonderful friend, but I'd much rather talk about you."

"Tom" and I spend the next hour laughing and talking, getting to know each other as though we were two people out on a first date. We share a chocolate shake, slice of apple pie, and several childhood stories. We talk about everything from our junior proms to the first time Drake/Tom got arrested. I ignore the other patrons in the diner when he moves from his side of the booth to mine and drapes an arm over my shoulder, and we make absolutely no move to leave until Jess drops off our bill and announces that the diner is closing.

"That was fun," I say, stepping out the front door.

We're on our way to Drake's car when he stops and looks at me.

"What would Bethany do if Tom wanted to hold her hand?"

I fight a grin, loving our little game. "I think she'd really like that."

Drake slips his hand in mine, linking our fingers together. The touch of his hand causes a spark of pleasure to zip through me—a visceral reaction so intense that I suck in a sharp breath.

"Are you okay?" he asks.

"Perfect." I tighten my fingers around his and lean into him as the crisp night air whips around us. Drake doesn't let me go until he's forced to.

"Your chariot awaits," he says, holding open the door.

I curtsey before climbing into his SUV. "Thank you, kind sir."

Drake jogs around the front of his Tahoe and hops in. Resting my head against the headrest, I close my eyes and savor the few moments I have alone with him. Our fingers find each other's on the center console, and I hold on, desperate for the night to continue. Because right now we may be Bethany and Tom, but we're also Drake and Abby.

The ride is quiet, and I'd like to think Drake is soaking up the moment the way I am.

"We're here."

When he announces our arrival at my place, my stomach plummets.

He releases my hand and puts the car in park, and I peel my eyes open. My apartment building is dark except for a small yellow light over the back door, barely giving off enough light to illuminate the parking spots. I'm not ready to go inside, but I know Drake has to work again tomorrow, and he needs to get some rest.

"Thank you for dinner and dessert."

"You're welcome."

Drake slides out of his vehicle at the same time I do and walks me to my door. For several seconds, I stand frozen, hoping he'll say *fuck it* and take me in his arms.

I imagine wrapping my legs around his waist as he pushes me against the door. He'll hoist me up, rip my panties off, and claim me the same way he did after Hannah's wedding reception.

The world would fall away as he filled me up, body and soul. I would get lost in him—lost in his touch and the steady beat of his heart against mine. But that fantasy is yanked out from under me when Drake places a chaste kiss on my cheek.

He's nothing if not gentle and upstanding.

"I'll see you around."

"Yeah, I'll see you around."

I slip inside, press my back against the door, and try to get my heart under control. When his vehicle starts up, I dash to the window, fling the curtain open, and watch him pull away. His taillights fade into the night, and I replay our evening over and over again—every laugh, every word, every touch—as I perform my nightly routine.

But it's not just tonight I'm thinking about; it's today in the OR, three days ago in my living room, and the twelve short hours we spent in his bed.

Flicking off my bedroom light, I crawl beneath the cool sheets and startle when my phone chimes from the nightstand.

I slide my finger across the screen and see a text.

Drake: Tom wanted nothing more than to kiss Bethany goodnight.

Me: Why didn't he?

I smile and watch three dots jump across my screen.

Drake: He wasn't sure if she was a kiss on the first date type of girl.

I bust up laughing.

Me: She is definitely not that type of girl. She is also firmly against one-night stands. Although I think she would've made an exception for Tom.

Drake: Why is that?

Me: Because Tom is special. She feels things when she's with him, things she's never felt. He scares her a little.

Drake: She has nothing to be scared of because Tom feels the same way about her. He would never hurt Bethany.

Me: Then maybe next time he should steal the kiss.

Drake: Will there be a next time? I hear Bethany is leaving soon to go back home.

Me: There better be. And plans can always be changed.

Those words fly onto the screen automatically, and it isn't until I press send that I realize the magnitude of what I just wrote.

I've always hated change, even though I need it. It makes me nervous and uncomfortable. But the thought of staying here longer doesn't give me a bit of anxiety. And the thought that I'd be doing it because of Drake is in and of itself a miracle.

But how would we make it work? Would he want to make it work? I wouldn't be able to extend my contract and stay at the hospital. I'd have to find a different job—one where Dr. Drake Merritt isn't my superior.

I swallow past the lump in my throat. What if I didn't find another job right away? I can't not work. And then if I did find another job, I'd have to go through orientation and get adjusted to a new position with new co-workers, and that makes me want to throw up.

There's a long pause, and instead of staring at my phone, I check my alarm clock to make sure it's set for tomorrow morning, and then I check it again, and twenty-seven times after that. I only stop checking it when my phone dings.

Drake: Goodnight, Abigail.

Me: Goodnight, Drake.

Chapter 7

Abby

The following week hurries by. I picked up two extra shifts on top of three I already had scheduled, which means I got to see Drake almost every day. Unfortunately, we didn't get to spend much time together. But we were able to steal a quick lunch twice and made plans for another dinner—one I was going to cook.

The lasagna and garlic bread were ready to go, and I'd just popped the cork on a bottle of wine when Drake messaged and said he wouldn't be able to make it. An emergency surgery stole our night together.

So I lit the candle in the middle of my kitchen table, plated dinner, and ate alone the way I have so many other nights in my life. That was two nights ago, and I haven't heard a word from Drake since.

Snow started to fall about two hours ago, toward the end of my final shift for the week, and it's accumulating much more quickly than I'd anticipated. On my way home, I stop by the hardware store to grab a pair of gloves. I'm standing in line to check out when a little girl carrying a plastic sled steps beside me with her dad close behind.

"Are you going to go sledding?" I ask, nodding toward the plastic disc.

The little girl nods her head, causing her blond curls to bounce. "My daddy is taking me. My brother broke my sled, so we had to get a new one."

"I've never been sledding. Is it fun?"

The little girl's eyes grow round. "You haven't?"

I shake my head.

"You hafta go! It's the most fun you'll ever have."

"She's right," her dad says. "I'm not afraid to admit I get as much enjoyment from flying down the hills as my kids do."

"No judgment here," I say, holding my hands up. "It sounds like a blast. I'm wondering if I shouldn't grab a sled for myself."

"They're back by the shovels," her dad says, nodding to my left.

"Where do people go sledding around here?"

"I own fifty acres on the outskirts of town, and we have some pretty good hills, so that's where we go. But when I was growing up, we used to go to the city park. There are a few hills out there."

For the life of me I can't remember seeing a park on my few short trips around town. "And where would I find the park?"

The girl's dad smiles. "Are you familiar with the town?"

"I know how to get to the coffee shop, book store, hospital, Abby's, and here."

"Abby's…" He shakes his head and looks down at his daughter before returning his attention to me. "I forgot all about that place. I don't think I've ever taken the kids out that way."

"You should. The burgers are to die for."

"I know. We used to go back in high school after the football games. And then I graduated, got married, had two kids, got divorced, and forgot all about it."

"Life always has a way of interfering in our plans, doesn't it?"

"That's an understatement."

"Abigail?"

I whirl around at the sound of my name. Drake is standing a few feet away, hands on his hips, and a frown marring his gorgeous face.

"Hey, stranger," I say. "What are you doing here?"

"Figured I should stock up on a few things with this storm coming in. What about you?" His eyes flit to the man and his daughter standing behind me.

"Realized I didn't have any gloves, so I stopped by to grab a pair, and I was just talking to this wonderful little girl and her father about Abby's." I turn to the side so he can get a look at the guy.

The man holds his hand out. "Drake Merritt, I haven't seen you in ages."

"Ben. It has been a while." Drake shakes the guy's hand but doesn't seem too pleased about it.

"I was just telling this beautiful young woman where she could find some good sledding hills."

Releasing Ben's hand, Drake looks at me. "You want to go sledding?"

"I was thinking about it. I've never been."

"I'll take you."

"You don't have to do that. I know how busy you've been." I really don't, though, since I haven't heard a word from him.

But in his defense, I haven't exactly gone out of my way to get ahold of him either, so I can't be all that upset.

Drake steps forward until he's all up in my personal space, which I don't mind one bit. The smell of sandalwood fills my nose, and all coherent thought flies out the window.

"I want to."

"Huh?"

"I want to take you sledding."

"Then we better buy a sled."

He nods and gives me a once over. "We also need to get you some warmer clothes and insulated boots."

* * * *

A hundred and twenty dollars and thirty minutes later, we're finally pulling into the city park. Per Drake's request, I followed him from the hardware store, and it's a damn good thing I didn't try to come here by myself because it was about ten different turns through six stoplights, and I'm certain I would've gotten lost. I pull into what I hope is a parking spot—who the hell can tell with this much snow on the ground—and pop my trunk.

I wore the snow pants and boots out of the store, so all I've got to put on are the gloves. When I grab a hat out of the bag in my trunk, Drake takes it from me.

"Are you attracted to that guy?" he says, pulling it over my ears.

I brush a strand of hair from my face and tuck it under the hat. "What guy?"

"Ben, from the hardware store."

"No, not at all. Why would you think that?"

Drake's shoulders relax, and his eyes soften. "Ben was always the most popular kid in school. All the guys wanted to be him, and the girls wanted to date him…including my girl."

"What? No!"

"Yes." Drake grabs my gloves and puts them on me while he continues to talk. "He even married her, although I think they're divorced now."

"They are," I confirm. "Were you jealous? Is that why you looked grumpy when you called out to me?"

"I was absolutely jealous," he says, closing what little distance there is between us. He strokes the back of his fingers down my cheek. "I've never been more jealous than I was when I walked in and saw you talking to Ben."

"Not even when your ex married him?"

Drake shakes his head. "Not even."

"Hmmm," I hum. "And here I thought you'd forgotten all about me this week."

"I could never forget about you. Trust me, I've tried."

I pout and Drake smooths his thumb over the wrinkle in my brow.

"I didn't mean that in a bad way. I just meant I've tried to stop lusting after you every time I look at you. My self-control is hanging on by a thread here lately, and I'm not sure how much longer I'll be able to keep my hands off of you."

"I'm not sure I'd stop you."

"I'm sorry I haven't called or texted you this week. Work has been crazy."

"You don't have to apologize, and you don't owe me an explanation."

"I know I don't, but I want to give it to you anyway. Every time I got the chance to message you, it was well after midnight, and I didn't want to wake you up. I kept telling myself I'd talk to you the next day at work, but then our paths never crossed or the day got away from me, and it was a vicious cycle."

"Drake." I take his hand in mine. "You don't have to explain. You forget that I have parents who are just as dedicated as you. I'm used to it. I promise it's okay."

"I'm not your parents."

"I know you're not."

"Do you?"

When I don't immediately answer, Drake closes his eyes as though he's trying to visualize what he wants to say. When he reopens them, they're filled with so much hope and longing that it nearly brings me to my knees.

"I keep trying to remind myself that you're leaving…that no matter how much I want something between us, I can't have it."

I want to tell him I don't have to leave and we can have whatever this is between us, but I'm not sure I'm ready for that yet. So instead, I cup his cheek in my hand.

"Let's not talk about this right now, okay? Right now, I just want to have fun. I want you to take me sledding."

"Is Tom taking Bethany out on a date?" He smiles crookedly, but it looks forced, and I hate it.

"No." I shake my head. "Today we're Drake and Abby, and this is whatever we want it to be."

Chapter 8

Drake

"Today we're Drake and Abby, and this is whatever we want it to be."

Abigail's words keep playing over and over in my head as I follow her up the giant hill. I tried to carry the sled, but she insisted, spouting off some bullshit about it being a rite of passage for her.

Whatever. I'm fucking helpless when it comes to this girl. I'd give her whatever the hell she needed or the shirt off my back if she asked for it, which is why I was determined to be the one to take her sledding when she voiced interest.

Now I'm determined to push her limits and see how far she's willing to bend. Last week when we were texting as Tom and Bethany, she mentioned a willingness to change her plans. At the time I wanted to ask her if she meant what she said, but if there's one thing I've learned about Abigail over the last couple of weeks, it's that she needs to take things slow, and I didn't want to push her. I thought if I sat back and let her take the lead, she'd show me where she wanted this to go.

But she didn't do a damn thing, and I started to think maybe she regretted what she said to me that night. Then a bit ago I saw the ache in her eyes when I told her how I want her and can't have her, and I heard longing in her voice when she said today we're Drake and Abby.

Now all I can think about is how different today would be if this were an actual date for Drake and Abby.

"So, if this is whatever we want it to be, does that mean it's a date?"

Abigail stops, the red plastic sled hoisted over her head, but doesn't turn around. "Is that what you want it to be?"

"Yes."

She seems to think about it for a second and then keeps climbing. "What if someone finds out?"

"How would anyone find out?" I ask, scooping up some snow. It's wet, not powdery—exactly how I like it.

"I don't know; I'm just asking."

"Are you going to tell anyone?"

She shakes her head. "No, but I'll want to. I see how the other nurses look at you."

"Now look who's jealous?" I tease.

"Oh, I'm not jealous."

"You're not, huh?"

"Nope, I don't get jealous. It's not part of my DNA."

"So you wouldn't be jealous if I told you I dated Farrah?"

Abigail gasps. She spins around just as I hurl the snowball I've been making, and it smacks her in the chest. Whatever she was about to say dies on her lips, which have formed a perfect little O.

"Did you just throw a snowball at me?"

"I did."

"I see." Dropping the sled to the ground, Abigail bends down and gathers a handful of snow. She starts forming a ball, and all I can do is laugh.

"Oh, sweetheart, you have no idea what you're starting. Remember, I'm from here. I've won more snowball fights than you—"

She nails me right in the nose with her tiny snowball and laughs out loud. Using my sleeve, I wipe the wetness from my face.

I scoop up more snow. "Three."

Abigail's smile fades.

"Two," I say, starting toward her.

She shrieks and runs up the hill as fast as her snowsuit and clunky boots will let her, sled be damned. She's so stinking cute, thinking she can get away from me.

"One."

I chuck the snowball. It hits her square in the back. She trips, falling into the snow, but quickly gets back up. She's laughing so hard I'm not sure how she's still running, but my girl doesn't stop. She disappears over the top of the hill and behind some trees.

"Abigail," I call, grabbing more snow. "Come out, come out wherever you are."

She doesn't make a peep, and I begin looking behind each of the trees. When I don't immediately find her, I kneel down and stockpile a few more snowballs, lifting the bottom of my coat to form a makeshift pocket. I stand up and turn to the trees when a blob of snow smacks the side of my face.

I blink away the snow in time to see Abigail fist-pump the air.

"It's on," I say, taking off after her. She turns and runs as I hit her with snowball after snowball. She dodges left, trying to lose me, but I'm too fast, and she's never run in this much snow. When I'm close enough, I tackle her to the ground as gently as possible. She rolls to her back. I straddle her hips, pinning her against the fluffy snow, and lift my arms in the air.

"All hail the snow king."

Abigail manages to grab a handful of snow and toss it in my face. She laughs when I snag her wrists, pinning them above her head.

"Say it."

"Say what?" she says, laughing harder.

"That I'm the snow king, ruler of the mountains and all people."

"Never."

I shift her wrists into one hand and slip my free hand under the hem of her coat. I tickle her side and Abigail's laugh gets louder as she tries to buck me off.

"Say it."

"Okay! Fine, you win."

"Not good enough. I want to hear you say it."

"You're the snow king, ruler of the mountains and all people! There, are you happy now?" she asks, trying to catch her breath.

It kills me to remove my hand from her soft skin, but I do. "Very."

Her nose and cheeks are red from the cold. Her hat is askew and some black waves have slipped out. I've never seen her look more beautiful than she does right now, and this time I'm not letting the moment pass me by.

I lean forward and kiss her smiling lips. Her mouth molds to mine, a soft moan rumbling deep in my throat. Our bodies seem to melt against the snow as Abigail fists the front of my coat in her hands, pulling me forward until my body covers hers.

My hard cock is pressed against her belly. I know she can feel it between the layers separating us because she shifts her hips, grinding them upward, and if we don't stop now, I'm going to blow my load like a horny teenager.

Abigail's grip on me loosens. Her hands reach for the bottom of my coat, but I capture them in mine, break the kiss, and rest my forehead against hers.

"Drake…" she breathes.

I could gather her in my arms and take her home right now—she wouldn't put up a fight. I can see it in her eyes. But I want to do this right, and I want to start by taking her sledding.

"Let me take you sledding, and then we'll go back to my place and get you warm. How does that sound?"

She nods and sits up enough to capture my mouth in another soft kiss. "I think that sounds like a great plan."

Chapter 9

Abby

"Mmm, that was so good."

I tilt my cup, finishing what's left of the hot cocoa Drake made me. As soon as we walked through his front door, he flipped a switch and his fireplace ignited, bathing the room in a soft orange glow. Warmth now seeps through me as I snuggle against the plush cushions of his couch.

"My fingers are finally starting to thaw out," I tell him.

After our kiss, Drake and I spent the next three hours sledding down four different hills, each one bigger than the last. I wiped out more times than I can count, got snow in places a girl shouldn't have snow, and had so much fun.

"I had a good time today," he responds.

"Me too." I smile over the rim of my mug.

"I would say we can do it again tomorrow, but I have to work."

I sigh. "I have to work tomorrow too. But maybe this weekend if the snow hangs around?"

"It's a date."

A date. Is that what today was? Am I breaking a company rule by dating Drake? My grip on the mug tightens, the hot cocoa curdling in the pit of my stomach.

"Abigail, breathe."

I suck in a breath I didn't realize I was holding and look at Drake. The need to ease my anxiety is growing by the second, and I'm afraid if I don't find a way to tamp it down, it's going to escalate, and I'll end up making an ass out of myself.

"Are you okay?" he asks.

"Fine."

"Really? Because you don't look so good."

I sit up on the couch and swallow. "My stomach is just unsettled, that's all."

"Is this because I said it's a date?"

"What? No." I shake my head a little too dramatically, but I can tell by the look on his face that he isn't buying it. "Okay, yes. Maybe a little."

He lifts a brow. "A little."

"Okay, a lot."

"Does the thought of us going on a date make you nervous? Because I considered today a date, and also the other night when I took you to Abby's."

"That was not a date."

"How do you figure?" His laughter lightens the mood, and I feel the knot in my stomach start to loosen. "I picked you up, drove you to a restaurant, bought you dinner and dessert, and walked you to your door. If that isn't a date, I don't know what is."

I grin. "You didn't kiss me at the end of the night."

"Trust me, I won't make that mistake again."

The promise of another kiss has my stomach tightening for a completely different reason. "It scares me."

"The kiss?"

"No," I laugh. "Us dating."

"You don't want to date. Do I stink?" he asks, lifting his arm and sniffing his shirt.

"Stop." I shove him playfully. "You don't stink."

"Then what's the problem?"

"It's against the rules. We're not supposed to date."

"Fuck the rules. This is our life," Drake declares. And then he leans in close, as if he's telling me a secret. "And the way I see it, some rules are meant to be broken. I like you, Abigail, more than I've ever liked another woman."

"I like you too, but I don't want you to risk your job because of me."

"Trust me, they're not going to fire me."

My eyes widen. "Then they'll fire me, and if that happens, I don't know what I'm going to do."

"They aren't going to fire you. I would never let that happen."

"I'm not sure you'd have much of a say."

"Abigail, I'm done pretending these feelings I have for you don't exist. You're only here for a short time, and I want to spend as much of it with you as possible."

"Drake—"

"I want more than work and stolen moments. I want this. I want to cuddle on the couch and take you sledding. I want to laugh with you and kiss you whenever I feel like kissing you."

"What happens when I leave?"

"I guess we'll have to cross that bridge when we come to it."

"Okay."

"Okay?"

"I want that too. The kisses, I mean. And the laughter and dates. Maybe you can take me snowshoeing."

Drake scoots closer to me on the couch. "I would love to take you snowshoeing."

"I'm probably going to suck at it."

"I don't care. Abigail?"

"Yes?"

"We're really going to do this?"

"If by this you mean break some rules and give in to this insane attraction to each other, then yes, we're really going to do this."

Drake takes the empty mug from my hands and sets it on the coffee table with his. And then he cups my face and takes my mouth in a heated kiss.

This kiss is so much more than the ones we shared at the park.

This kiss holds promises of what's to come. Threading my fingers through his hair, I pull him close. His hands fall to my hips. He lifts me up to straddle his lap, and not once do we break the kiss.

* * * *

Drake

"Wait, Abigail."

She pulls her lips from mine and looks down at me. "What's wrong?"

Her hair falls forward, creating the perfect curtain. I push my fingers through her soft locks so I can see her beautiful face. "Nothing is wrong, but I don't want to do this here."

A shy smile tugs at the corner of her mouth, but her words are much more brazen. "Then I suggest you take me back to your room."

She shrieks when I lift her into my arms and stride purposefully down the hall. I kick open my bedroom door and position her on the center of my bed. She reaches for me, but I pull back. Hooking my fingers in the sides of her pants, I give them a little tug. Abigail lifts her hips, and I slide her pants, along with her panties, down her legs and toss them aside. Her shirt and bra are the next things to go, and when she's lying naked in front of me, I nearly swallow my tongue.

"You're so beautiful."

I've seen her naked before, but it was through the eyes of a man who had to say goodbye the next morning. I felt rushed, desperate to touch every inch of her body before sunrise because I knew I'd never get to touch this angel again.

Except here she is. Dark hair fanned out over my pillow, cheeks still pink from our time in the snow, and lips puffy from my kiss. My heart squeezes tight at the sight of her.

"Drake, I need you to touch me."

"Getting to that, sweetheart."

I peel my shirt over my head, kick my pants and boxers off, and lean down to press my lips to the center of her belly. I kiss my way up her body—across her chest, up her neck, and when I hit the soft spot below her jaw, Abigail arches her head against the pillow and sighs my name.

God, that's the best sound in the world.

My cock is hard as steel against her stomach, pre-cum forming on the tip. She wiggles her hand between our bodies, wraps her delicate fingers around my cock, and I groan against her.

"Careful, I'm barely hanging on."

I take one of her nipples into my mouth until she's writhing beneath me.

"I don't want you hanging on," she pants. "I want you to let go."

She guides me to her entrance and tries to put me inside of her, but I pull back—though not because I need a condom; we had that talk the first time we were together.

"Wait, Abigail. If I push inside right now, I'm going to lose it before we even get started. That's how worked up you've got me."

"I don't care. I just need you, Drake. Please."

"You don't ever have to beg, Abigail. You know I'll give you whatever you want. I'd give you the whole damn world if you'd let me," I add, a husky plea against her silky skin.

I'm not even sure if she heard me between her soft moans. She lines the head of my cock against her entrance, hooks a leg around my hip, and tosses her head back when I push inside.

"Oh, God," she pants. "I forgot how good you feel."

"I don't ever want you to forget me, Abigail. God, baby, this is going to be quick, but I promise next time we'll take it slow."

Her lips part, but all that comes out is a deep groan when I surge inside of her. I capture her lips with mine and start moving, relishing the feel of our connection—her hands gripping my back as though she's afraid I'll disappear, her heels digging into my ass, and the way her mouth claims mine while I push her body toward the edge.

She lifts her hips. My body moves of its own accord, and I pound into her. Her body constricts around mine, and I know she's getting close. I press my thumb to her clit and rub in tight, small circles until she closes her eyes and digs her head into my pillow.

"Look at me, Abigail. I want to see those beautiful eyes when you come undone."

Her eyelids pop open, and I feel drugged. Hypnotized by her body and soul. Hyperaware of all things Abigail.

"Drake, I'm...I..."

"I've got you, sweet girl."

I rub her clit and pump my hips as the pressure in my body builds. There's a tingling deep in my gut, radiating to my spine. I know she feels it too because her hips become more erratic, meeting mine thrust for thrust as we chase our orgasms. Our climax hits at the same time, zaps of pleasure pushing toward my arms and legs, down to my toes. It's all-consuming, and the best damn orgasm I've ever had.

Abigail screams and her body tightens, pulsing around me as I spill inside of her. I thrust several more times, bury my face in her neck, and groan as her body goes lax beneath mine.

"Abigail," I breathe.

There's no response, just the feel of her fingers in my hair as she holds me to her. We lie like this for several minutes, both of us trying to catch our breath as our bodies float down from the ultimate high.

When I regain a little strength, I lift my head and look into her eyes. They're clearer than they've ever been. There isn't much I wouldn't do to have them shining back at me every day. I'd give up just about anything to erase the expiration date between us.

Except it's not that easy.

Or is it?

My grandfather always used to tell me life is what you make it. If you want something, go after it. Make it happen.

"Stay in Cunningham Falls," I blurt.

She laughs, and my semi-erect cock slips from her body. "Wait. You're serious?"

"Yes. I feel something for you, Abigail. Something strong, something I've yet to feel for another woman, and I think you feel it too."

She nods. "I do."

"I don't know about you, but I want to keep exploring this, because I think it could grow into something great."

Her eyes fill with tears. "I do too."

"Stay. Tell me you'll stay."

"What about work?"

I blow out a breath and sit up, pulling her with me. Reaching toward the bottom of the bed, I grab the blanket that slipped off and pull it around us.

"We'll figure something out. Maybe when your contract is over you can find something else in the area."

She bites on her bottom lip and nods, but doesn't look convinced. I cup her face in my hands and bring my lips to hers.

"I don't have all the answers, but I promise if you stay, we'll figure something out. Something that works for both of us."

Soft hands wrap around my neck, playing with the hair on the nape of my neck. She rests her forehead to mine and smiles. "Okay."

"Really?" I pull back, needing to get a good look at her, needing to make sure she's here and this is real. "You'll stay?"

She nods again and laughs when I tackle her back to the bed.

"I'll call the agency tomorrow and see if they can find something for me here after my contract."

"And if they can't?" I ask.

"We'll figure something out. Now, I do believe you promised me a next time."

Chapter 10

Abby

"I think you broke me," I say, collapsing on the bed. "I won't be able to walk for days."

"The way I see it, you'll have a reminder of me with every step you take."

I poke him in the side. Drake squirms and grabs my hand, pulling it to his lips. He kisses each knuckle before placing my hand against his chest.

"I should get going. It's getting late, and we have to be at work in—" I look at the alarm clock and groan. "—six hours."

"Stay," he says.

"The night?"

He grins. "Yes."

"I can't."

"Why not?"

"I don't know." I laugh, pushing up to an elbow so I can look at him more easily. "I've never stayed the night with a man before."

"You stayed with me after Hannah's wedding."

"You're right." I grin. "That was my first time."

Grabbing my wrist, he pulls me to his chest. "I like being your first. Say yes."

My head is screaming at me to go home, that this is a bad idea. I don't have a change of clothes or my lunch, which means I'll have to go home before work in the morning. I'll probably be rushed, and if my day starts that way, it'll only continue. But my heart doesn't seem to care. My heart says live a little. My heart says *stay*.

"Yes. But you have to promise not to tempt me with your seductive ways. I need all the sleep I can get, or I'll be a bear in the morning."

Drake lifts me from his chest and jumps out of bed. He grabs a shirt from his closet and pulls it over my head.

"What're you doing?" I ask, slipping my arms into the soft cotton. It smells like Drake—clean and woodsy and oh so yummy.

"I really hate to cover this gorgeous body, but if I don't, neither one of us will sleep."

I bury my nose in the material and take a giant sniff. "You're never getting this shirt back."

Drake grabs my hand and pulls me up. "It's yours, but I still get to touch it anytime I'd like, right?"

"You better."

"You're going to regret saying that," he says, slapping my ass. "Let's go brush our teeth. I've got a spare toothbrush."

We brush our teeth side by side. He props a hip on the doorframe and watches me wash away what's left of my makeup. It feels so natural to do these mundane tasks with him—and also a little exciting.

When we get back to his bedroom, I crawl into his California king and reach for the alarm clock.

"The time is already set. You just have to turn it on," he says, crawling in beside me.

I believe him, but I have to check it for myself. I press the alarm button, check the time, and flip the switch to ON. And then I check the time again to make sure I didn't accidentally set it for PM instead of AM. After the third time checking it, Drake drags me to bed.

"Get over here and kiss me goodnight," he says, capturing my lips.

All thoughts of the alarm clock and getting up on time evaporate as his tongue pushes against mine. By the time we come up for air, I'm practically climbing him like a tree, and I'm seconds away from begging him to rip this shirt off and fuck me again, sleep be damned.

Instead, Drake situates the pillow, flips off the light, and pulls me into his arms.

"Goodnight, Abigail."

"Goodnight."

His arms are warm and soft wrapped around me, and the steady rise and fall of his chest against my body is so very soothing. After only a few minutes, Drake's breathing becomes slow and steady.

"Did you lock the front door?" I ask before he has a chance to doze off.

"Mmm-hmm."

"And the back door?"

"Mmm-hmm," he mumbles again.

"Because I opened the patio door to look outside earlier when we first got here."

"They're both locked."

Drake must sense my unease because he wraps his hand around mine and says, "Would you like me to go check to be sure?"

"No, you don't have to do that."

"I don't mind."

I kiss his hand. "I know you don't. Thank you for offering, though."

"Go check if you need the reassurance. But I promise I would never let anything happen to you, and I promise I will never tell you I'm sure about something unless I'm one hundred percent sure."

"Okay." I nod and settle myself in the crook of his arm. I don't say another word, and about the time Drake's breathing evens back out, I reach over and check the alarm one last time. And then I check it seven more times just to be certain, and when I curl back up to Drake's body, he rests a hand on my hip.

"Is it good?"

"It's good."

"Great. Now get some sleep, sweetheart."

* * * *

"I called you last night," Hannah says, sliding onto a seat across from me.

"You did?" I shove a french fry into my mouth.

"Yup. Twice."

"Hmm... I'm not sure how I missed it." Lies. All lies. I probably didn't hear it because I was screaming Drake's name, begging him to fuck me harder. Except I can't tell her that. Not yet at least.

"And when you didn't answer, I went to your house."

Oh shit.

I take another fry and chew it slowly. "Is that so?"

She nods. "Want to tell me where you were?"

"Not really."

Hannah waits a few seconds and then rolls her eyes. "Jesus Christ, Abigail, I know you're banging Drake. Just admit it already."

Her voice is a little loud, and I hold a finger to my lips. "Would you keep it down?"

"Damn it, Abby, we used to tell each other everything. And Drake's one of my best friends. Why would you keep this from me?"

She actually looks a little hurt, and I immediately feel bad.

"I'm sorry, Han. It's not that I didn't want to tell you; it just sorta happened fast, and you and I haven't spent a lot of time together for me to tell you."

"So it's true?"

I nod. "How did you figure it out?"

"Besides the fact that I could feel the attraction between you every time you were within ten feet of each other?"

"Yes, besides that."

"When you weren't home, I drove to his house on a hunch. Your car was in the driveway."

"Hannah Hull, were you spying on me?"

She blinks innocently. "I wouldn't call it spying. It's more like looking out for you."

"Well, you don't have to look out for me. I'm a big girl now."

"Will you at least tell me how it happened? But, please, leave out the sexual details because he's one of my best friends, and I really don't need to hear about how horrible he is in bed or how little his dick is."

"Oh, trust me, he's not horrible. In fact, he's amazing. And his dick is—"

"Nope," she hollers, shaking her head vehemently. "TMI. Let's stick to the very basic details."

"Fine. Remember at your wedding reception when you were telling me I need to take more chances?" Hannah nods. "And then do you remember Grace telling me I should start by having a one-night stand with a stranger? Well, I had a one-night stand, and Drake was the stranger."

"You're telling me you and Drake have been canoodling since my wedding reception and you've kept it from me this whole time?"

"Canoodling, Hannah? What are we, seventy?"

"You know what I mean."

"No, we haven't been canoodling. It really was just a one-night stand until I moved here."

"Now what?" she asks. "Are you two dating? What's going to happen when you leave?"

I shrug. "I don't know if we're dating. I think we might be. We haven't exactly put a label on it. And...I might not be leaving so soon after all."

"What?" she shrieks. "You're staying? If I'd known Drake is what would get you to move here for good, I would've introduced you two a long time ago."

I roll my eyes. "I have plans of calling the agency on my next day off to see what we can work out. I need to see if they can get me placed at a different hospital."

"Why can't you stay here? Farrah told me you're doing wonderfully, and everyone loves you."

"That's really great to hear, but Drake and I are breaking some pretty serious rules by seeing each other. And if we're going to try to make it work, I want to do it the right way, and that means no sneaking around."

"Oh." She frowns. "I didn't even think about the non-fraternization policy. But I agree one hundred percent. Sneaking around would suck. There's no way I would've been able to sneak around with Brad. He's too edible, and I can barely keep my hands off of him."

"Trust me, it's a struggle. Especially when he walks by me in those damn scrubs. His ass is so tight. I just want to push him into the supply closet and—"

"That's enough," Hannah says, standing up. "We're going to have to set some serious boundaries when we talk about Drake and the things you want to do to him."

"Dirty things. I want to do lots of dirty, filthy things."

"Not listening," she sings, walking away.

"But nothing he hasn't already done to me," I holler.

"I can't hear you."

Chapter 11

Abby

And that's exactly how I spend the next week: doing lots of dirty, filthy things with Drake. Sometimes he does them to me, other times I do them to him, and in between all the dirty, we have lots of fun.

Like today, for example. Drake decided to take me snowshoeing, since the snow hung around longer than expected. It was a lot easier than I had anticipated, and I think I was pretty good at it. I even asked Drake how I did, but he mauled me the way he does every time we walk through the door, and here we are.

"Next time, we've got to make it to the bedroom. I'm getting too old for living-room-floor sex," he says, dropping his head back against the hardwood floor.

We barely made it into the house before his mouth was on mine. He stripped me down, and I'd just gotten his pants around his knees when he was surging inside of me.

"You know that's never going to happen. We're better off replacing your hardwood with some nice, plush carpet."

"That'll work too," he says, slapping my ass.

I jump up, grab the T-shirt he tossed aside, and tug it over my head. "I'm going to make some hot chocolate. Want some?"

"Sure." He reaches out a hand, and I help pull him off the floor, admiring just how handsome he is.

Drake might not do physical labor at his job, but he puts in time at the gym, and it pays off. His chest is rock solid, his abs are cut into deep rivulets, and then there's that perfect little V I'd only read about in romance novels. I always thought they were somewhat of a unicorn—something most men only strive for, but never get. I was wrong. They are real.

Very, very real.

"Keep looking at me like that, and you'll be flat on your back with my cock inside you again."

My cheeks flush as I watch Drake hike his pants up. He leaves them unbuttoned, and I'm tempted to just throw my naked body at him and tell him to do his worst. But I'm cold, and my vagina is sore.

Also something I didn't know could actually happen.

"I'm keeping this shirt," I say, pulling the soft cotton to my nose.

Drake laughs, plops down on the couch, and reaches for the remote. "You say that every time you put one on."

"You think I'm kidding. I'm not." Turning on my heel, I head for the kitchen to make our hot chocolate. When I return a few minutes later, Drake is watching the evening news.

"Here you go."

He takes the mug of cocoa. "Thank you."

I snuggle up beside him on the couch and watch the news. When the anchor reports on a house fire, my mind instantly jumps to the stove.

Did I turn it off?

I'm sure I did, but I don't remember doing it.

I set my mug down, and Drake mutes the TV. "Where are you going?"

"To check the stove. I can't remember if I turned it off."

When I get into the kitchen and see the kettle sitting on the back burner, I'm relieved. I can also see that the knob is in the off position, but I touch it anyway, making sure it's there, and then I hover my hand above the stove to see how much heat it's producing. There's a little warmth coming off the burner, but not much, so I check the knob another three times (just for good measure), and to reassure myself, I say it out loud.

"The stove is off."

My mom used to tell me the way I talk to myself is silly, but for me it's a comforting measure. Later on when I start to worry about the stove again—and I will worry about it—I'll remember saying it out loud. It'll be a reminder that I've already checked it and don't need to check it again.

So, it might be silly, but it works.

"The stove is off."

By the time I make it back to the living room, my cocoa isn't so hot, and Drake is watching me. The TV is still on mute, and when I sit down, he clears his throat.

"Can I ask you a question?"

Here it is. I knew this conversation was coming, and it's probably something we should've talked about much sooner than now.

"You can ask me anything."

"Have you ever been evaluated for your OCD?"

I take a breath, and Drake shakes his head.

"I'm sorry. I hope that didn't come off as rude. I didn't mean anything bad by it; it's just that I've noticed some OCD traits. I've wanted to ask a few times, but I—"

"Drake." I stop him by covering his hand with mine. "It's okay. You don't have to apologize. My anxiety causes me to be embarrassed in certain situations, but I'm not embarrassed by my OCD. Most people are more uncomfortable talking about it than I am."

"Will you talk to me about it?"

I nod and finish off my cocoa. Drake takes the cup and sets it on the coffee table.

"My parents worked a lot, which meant I spent a lot of time at home by myself. One morning—I think I was in junior high—I left for school and forgot to unplug the curling iron. My dad was pissed. He yelled and screamed, said I was lucky I didn't burn the house down. Every day after that, I started checking and double checking myself. It all sort of escalated from there. Did I shut the refrigerator all the way? Did I unplug the curling iron? Did I shut off the stove? Did I turn out the lights? Did I set my alarm? Did I lock the doors? My parents started to notice and took me to see one of their friends who was a child psychologist. I didn't meet the guidelines for a formal diagnosis."

"Really?"

"Shocking, I know."

"I'm sorry. It's just that you seem to have a lot of the symptoms."

"I do, but I'm able to control them if I try hard enough. For most patients with OCD, their obsessions, compulsions, or both aren't easily controlled."

"How do you control yours?"

"It's hard to explain."

"Will you try? I'm genuinely curious."

I think about it for a second and then put it into words as best I can. "When I'm doing what I call rituals: checking my alarm, the lock on the front door, or the refrigerator—"

"Sponges in the surgical room?"

I smile. "That too. When I'm checking those things over and over again, I know I'm being irrational. In my head, I realize I've already checked it, but it's difficult to stop. It's almost like I get anxious, and I keep doing the ritual until the anxiety subsides. Sometimes I'll check something two or three times and sometimes thirty."

"Wow."

"Thirty is a little excessive. I haven't been that obsessive in a few years."

"How many times did you just check the stove?"

"Four."

"Why four? Is that a special number for you?"

I shrug. "No. It just felt right."

Drake looks amazed. "Do you have triggers?"

I nod. "Change. I don't do well with change."

"But you moved here; that was a huge change."

"It has been." I clench my hands into fists, release them, and then blurt out what I've been wanting to tell Drake since I moved here. "And you gave me the push I needed."

"Me?" He points to himself, and I nod.

"Before I came here I was complacent—in a rut, so to speak. I was doing the same thing day in and day out. Consistency causes some of my rituals to diminish. When I'm comfortable, the anxiety isn't as bad. And I loved it. I felt freed from the one thing that always seemed to be holding me back."

"So you secluded yourself?"

"In a way," I answer. "I still had close friends I spent time with, but I avoided meeting new people and new situations in my personal life. My therapist said I was actually hurting myself, and if I wasn't careful I would turn into a recluse."

"And you don't want that?"

"Not at all. Hannah has been trying to get me to move here, but I was scared to make such a big change. I wanted to make it... In my heart I wanted to be closer to her and push my boundaries, but I couldn't pull the trigger...until you."

"Why me?"

"When you came up to me that night at the bar, I thought I was going to throw up all over your white shirt." Drake laughs and I find myself laughing along with him. "I'm serious. I was so scared, and then..."

Smiling, I look down at my hands and then into Drake's warm, brown eyes. They're as kind today as when I met him, and even though they still smolder when they look at me, tonight they're softer.

"And then..." he prompts.

"And then you made me laugh—over and over again. And I think I made you laugh too."

"You did."

"That hadn't happened to me in a long time. I kept waiting for the doubt and insecurities to creep in, but though they were simmering below the surface, they never boiled over."

"God, Abigail, I feel like such an ass."

"What? Why?"

"Because I kept flirting with you, and then I pushed you to dance when you didn't want to—"

I shake my head. "No, I'm glad you did. You pushed me further than I thought I could go, and then you kissed me, and something inside of me exploded."

"What do you mean?"

"It's like my brain moves at warp speed. I'm constantly thinking about what I'm going to do next, and will it cause me anxiety, and how I'm going to relieve that anxiety—will I count or resort to checking? Will it be the thing that finally pushes me over the edge? Most of the time, my thoughts are a complete blur."

Drake is sitting on the edge of the couch, watching me as though he sincerely cares about me and what I'm feeling. Scratch that, I *know* he cares about me, and that's why it's easy to tell him everything, because I know he won't judge me or laugh.

"And then you kissed me, and the blur I'd gotten so used to living in was gone. It was just me and you. It was your lips against mine and the touch of your hand on my back. It was the steady beat of your heart and the way you held me. Nothing else mattered. I didn't care about anything else in that moment except you."

I barely get the last word out of my mouth before Drake has me on his lap. My knees are pressed to the couch on either side of his hips. I run my fingers up his chest and link them at the back of his neck.

"I felt the same way," he whispers, his lips brushing mine. "You scared the shit out of me. When I saw you from across the room, it was like the floor had been ripped out from under me. I followed you to the bar, and next thing I knew you were laughing."

"What happened when I laughed?"

Drake kisses me softly at first and then with more passion. His tongue pushes into my mouth, tangling with mine. He swallows my moans and when we finally part, I'm breathing hard and Drake looks like he could slay a dragon.

"When you laughed, I fell. And I've been falling ever since."

"Drake."

"I know it's soon. I realize we haven't been dating long, but I'm falling, Abigail. My dad always told me, '*When you know, you just know.*' I was a little skeptical of that theory, until I met you."

"I feel the same way."

Drake's lips part, his eyes round with wonder. "You do?"

Laughing, I nod and kiss him. "Yes."

Next thing I know I'm cradled in Drake's arms as he strides down the hallway with purpose.

"Where are we going?"

"I need more than words right now. I need to show you how I feel."

"Oooh. I like where this is going. Will there be touching?"

He kicks his bedroom door open, tosses me on the bed, and crawls up my body. "Lots and lots of touching," he says, following each word with a kiss.

He starts at my belly and works his way up, undressing me along the way.

"And kisses?"

"Lots of kisses. And if I'm doing it right, lots of moans and sighs."

"What the hell are we waiting for?"

Chapter 12

Abby

"What are you doing?" I whisper as Drake drags me into an empty room along a hospital corridor.

He pushes me up against the wall and presses the sweetest kiss to my lips.

"Are you crazy?" I laugh, squirming away.

"For you."

"Come on, Drake, seriously. You can't do this. What if someone catches us?"

"No one's going to catch us."

"You don't know that. Any of the other nurses could've seen us slip in here."

Drake puts a hand on the wall beside my head and leans in close enough that I can feel his breath on my face. "I missed you," he says, placing a kiss to the base of my neck.

"You've seen me a hundred times today."

He shakes his head. "Not enough."

Damn it. Why does he have to be so sweet?

"My lips miss yours. They demanded I steal a kiss."

"Well, you've stolen one. Now get back to work. Go save someone's life or something." I try to push him away, except he doesn't budge.

Warm lips capture mine in another gentle kiss. "There, I stole two. And don't pretend you didn't like it."

"I did like it." I smile, slipping under his arm.

I manage to escape his wandering hand, and when he slaps my ass, I shriek and bolt out of the room, only to run into my charge nurse.

Drake's hand snaps out, catching her before she falls over.

"Oh, God, I'm so sorry. Are you okay?" I ask.

She shrugs Drake off and looks between us several times before nodding. "I'm fine. What were you two doing in there?"

"Oh, uh…"

"Discussing a patient." Drake dips his hands into his pockets.

Cindy's eyes narrow, and I know right away she doesn't believe him. I mean, why on Earth would we walk to the end of the hall and discuss a patient in an empty room? We could've talked in a number of different places, and this isn't one of them.

Shit.

"I was looking for you," Cindy says, her eyes narrowed on me. "Room 212 needs a dressing change."

"That's my patient. I'll assist." Drake puts a hand to my elbow to guide me away.

Cindy steps in front of us, blocking me. She looks from Drake to me and back to Drake, who looks pissed. His face is as hard as stone, and when he lifts a brow, silently daring her to challenge him, Cindy backs down. She steps to the left, allowing us to pass.

My heart slams inside my chest, and I pick up my pace, needing to get away from Drake for a few seconds, because clearly I can't think when I'm around him.

Why did I allow him to pull me into that room? I know better than that. *He* knows better than that.

"Slow down," he says softly. "You're drawing attention to yourself."

"I think we drew attention to ourselves when you pulled me into that room," I whisper-hiss.

"Abigail, it's fine."

"Really? Because I don't think so. And this is my job, Drake. I need the money."

"Your job is fine. I told you I would never let anything happen to you."

We stop in front of room 212. The patient is on contact precautions, so as soon as I walk through the door, I pull a gown off the cart and slip it on. Drake reaches for one as well, and I shake my head.

"No," I whisper. "I don't need you in here. I think right now it's best if we're not seen together."

Drake flinches as though my words deliver an actual blow. He doesn't say a word, just watches me don my mask and gloves, and then I slip around the privacy curtain.

Twenty minutes later, when I return to the hallway, he's gone. Not that I expected him to still be standing there.

The rest of the shift is nonstop busy, which is a blessing, and not once do I catch another glimpse of Drake. Three discharges, two direct admits, and a code blue in room 236 keep me hopping, and I don't have time to think about what happened earlier, let alone analyze it.

Four o'clock rolls around, and I collapse in a chair at the nurse's station. Twelve-hour shifts don't bother me, but today, my feet are on fire, and I've still got three hours to go.

"Abby."

I'm so used to Drake calling me Abigail that the shortened version of my name almost sounds funny, which is why I'm laughing when I say, "Yeah?" And then I nearly choke when I see Cindy standing at the desk.

"Can you come with me?"

"Oh, uh, yeah." I shut the chart and put it back on the rack. "If this is about Drake—"

"This isn't a discussion we'll be having at the nurse's station, Ms. Darwin."

Oh, hell. She used my last name.

Cindy turns on her heel and stops beside Farrah. "I'm going to need you to cover Abby's patients for a few minutes."

Farrah nods, her eyes darting to mine. I look away and follow Cindy down two halls and a flight of stairs to a familiar room. It's the room I came to for my four-hour orientation on my first day here. She opens the door, motioning for me to enter. The first thing I notice is the head of Human Resources—Sarah, I think her name is—perched at the end of a small conference table.

She's wearing a crisp black pantsuit, and her red heels are crossed at the ankle. "Please, have a seat, Ms. Darwin."

I turn, and that's when my eyes land on the other person in the room.

Drake.

He's sitting in a chair on the opposite side of the table, and when he looks up at me, I know whatever is about to happen isn't going to be good.

My stomach falls to my feet. I nearly trip on it walking into the room.

My legs feel like Jell-O as I walk across the small space and take a seat next to Drake. Except I don't dare look at him. Cindy shuts the door quietly, and she and Sarah sit across from us.

Sarah's smile is warm as she slides a binder across the table and taps it with a manicured nail.

"Do you know what this is, Ms. Darwin?"

"Yes, ma'am. It's the company handbook," I answer.

She flips open the cover and points to the front page. "And is that your signature stating that you received a copy of the handbook and reviewed it?"

"Yes, ma'am."

Sarah nods and pulls the binder back. "Do you know why I called you in here today?"

It doesn't even cross my mind to lie. That's not who I am, and though I've been acting out of the norm lately, there are some things that won't change. "I believe so, yes."

Her eyes shift to Drake's, and I feel the slightest weight lift from my shoulders. But the relief is momentary, because when she pulls her gaze back to mine, it's at full force.

"I'm going to be blunt, Ms. Darwin. Are you and Dr. Merritt in a romantic relationship?"

"Yes."

"And you're aware of the company's non-fraternization policy?"

"I am."

"And you're familiar with the policy, Dr. Merritt?" she asks, sliding her eyes one seat over.

Drake's jaw pops. "Yes, of course I'm familiar."

"Unfortunately, we only have one way to proceed. We refuse to break policy, which means one of you will be let go." She angles herself toward me. "It'll have to be Ms. Darwin."

"No, absolutely not," Drake declares. "Abigail is a wonderful nurse. She shouldn't lose her job because of a mistake we both made."

The air is sucked from my lungs as I hear Drake describe what we've shared as a mistake.

"These rules are in place for a reason, Dr. Merritt, and our non-fraternization policy is not negotiable. It isn't enforced on a case-by-case basis." Sarah sighs. "As for Abby, I agree with you. She has been an asset to this hospital. Cindy has had nothing but good things to say about her, and we will be sad to see her leave, but the alternative is letting you go, and that's not going to happen. But frankly, Dr. Merritt, I'm disappointed in you. You're in a position of authority. You know better than this," she scolds.

I half expect Drake to have some sort of comeback, except he doesn't. His lips snap shut. All of the emotion drains from his face as he stares off into nothing. For a brief second, I wonder what he's thinking, and then my mind takes over.

What the heck am I going to do now? How will this affect my contract with the agency? Will they let me go? Will this affect any future jobs I try to get?

Oh, God. This is going to follow me around for the rest of my career. I'm forever going to be the girl who slept with a supervisor. I'll be criticized and judged at every turn.

Bile rushes up my throat, and I try to swallow it down, but it's useless. My body goes on autopilot. I look up at the ceiling and start counting as the conversation carries on around me. I can feel the weight of someone's stare. I don't have to look to know it's Drake. I can tell by the hairs on the back of my neck that are standing on end. But I refuse to break my concentration.

I count forty-two tiles before his voice penetrates the fog in my head.

"You're right. I do know better. It was wrong of us to continue a relationship, knowing it was against policy. I assure you we will no longer date while I'm in a position of authority over her."

My stomach twists, and it's a good thing I'm sitting down because otherwise I would've doubled over at the pain. How could he say that after everything we've been through? After all the talks we've had, and after I asked my supervisor at the agency about staying longer? Son of a bitch, didn't we just talk about how we were falling for each other? And now we're a *mistake*, and he pretty much just ended our relationship?

Did he get his fill of me? Maybe I was a fun fling, but at the first sign of trouble, he's bailing. I never would've pegged Drake as that kind of guy.

"But," he says, catching my attention. "I will ask that you consider letting her finish her contract."

Is he nuts? He must be if he thinks I'll continue to work here—beside him—after we break things off. They might as well can my ass, because there's no way in hell I can stay longer now.

"Dr. Merritt—"

"Just hear me out."

I wait for Drake to continue, and when he doesn't, I look at him. Lifting a brow, I silently urge him on. *Please, let's hear your suggestion, Dr. Merritt.*

Drake frowns and then turns to Sarah. "I would like to talk with Phillip."

"Who's Phillip?" I ask.

"The administrator," he says without looking at me. "Let Abby go, call Phillip, and we'll discuss my suggestion."

What I want to say is, *what suggestion?* But I'm consumed by the fact that he just called me Abby.

Drake hasn't called me Abby once. Ever.

A sharp pain stabs the center of my chest. I've had friends tell me how much love sucks, but I never believed them until now. I guess I always looked at love as a positive thing—two people caring for each other through thick and thin, someone to spend time with and share secrets and dreams with. I never thought much about the other side of love—about what happens when one half of the whole gives up.

Screw falling… I've smacked the ground face first.

I love Drake Merritt.

Perfect fucking timing, Abigail.

"Abby?"

I blink up at Sarah. "Yes?"

"I said you can go. Please report to my office at the beginning of your next scheduled shift."

I should tell her no, that she can fire me right now. Hell, I'll even make it easy for her and quit. At this point I don't care if the agency cans me as well. I just want my boring apartment and boring old routine back.

Unfortunately, my feet don't pay much attention to my head, and instead of saying I quit, I haul ass out the door.

Chapter 13

Abby

I blow a chunk of hair from my eyes and sit back on my haunches, inspecting my work. I've spent the last three hours cleaning every square inch of this apartment while I wait for my contact at the agency to return my call. At this time of the evening, I half expect not to hear from her, but when I called in a complete panic, they assured me she would call me back tonight.

Until then, I've been doing everything I can to kill time. I've scrubbed the bathrooms as well as the kitchen, pulled everything out of the perfectly stocked cabinets only to put it all right back in, and I've packed all of my clothes in the hopes that she'll give me the news I want to hear.

The first hour I was home dragged on. At first, I hoped Drake would barge through my front door to tell me everything I heard come out of his mouth was a complete lie. He would declare his undying love for me and sweep me off my feet, and we'd live happily ever after.

Except those are the very best scenes of fairy tales. This is real life, and no matter how bad I wish Drake to be my prince charming, he's not.

I haven't heard a word from him. Not a text or phone call.

The phone rings, and I drop the scrub brush I'm using to clean the baseboards and dart across the room to grab it.

"Hello?"

"Abby, it's Melanie. I got your message. What's going on?"

"I need you to get me out of here."

She laughs. "What are you talking about? Just the other day you begged me to find a way to extend your time in Montana."

"I know. I was delusional. I want out. In fact, I'd really like to go back home. This traveling thing isn't for me. I thought I could do it, but I can't—"

"Slow down. First things first. There's a contract in place, and I can't just break it. But I've yet to find you something else in Montana to accommodate the extension you asked for, so I'm sure it won't be a problem getting you home."

"Great," I sigh, walking toward the bedroom.

"After your contract is up."

"What? No. You don't understand; I can't stay here." I vaguely hear the sound of a door opening and closing, but I'm too preoccupied, and I've got a one-track mind. "I need you to get me the hell out of here. I want out of Cunningham Falls and far away from Montana."

Melanie says something, but I don't hear because the phone disappears from my hand.

"Hey!" I whirl around to find Drake glaring at me.

"What the fuck are you doing?" he asks, holding my cell in the air.

How dare he barge in here and talk to me like that? I square my shoulders and lift my chin. "I'm going home."

"So I heard." He shakes his head. "I can't believe you were going to bail without even talking to me."

My eyes widen. "Talk to you? It's funny you'd want that courtesy after breaking things off between us without talking to *me* first."

"*What?*" He has the audacity to look completely confused. "What the hell are you talking about? I didn't break things off with you."

"Jesus Christ, Drake, I'm not deaf." I yank my phone from his hand. "I was sitting right there. First you called what we had a *mistake*, and then you said, and I quote, '*It was wrong of us to continue a relationship, knowing it was against policy. I assure you we will no longer date while I'm in a position of authority over her.*'"

Drake's jaw drops. A couple of seconds later, he snaps it shut. "This is a fucking joke," he mumbles.

Pushing his fingers into his hair, he turns and takes a few steps.

"After last night, after everything we shared…" Hands on his hips, he looks at the floor. "I can't believe you're doing this."

"I'm not doing anything," I shout, stepping in front of him. If he wants to accuse me of screwing this up, he's going to do it to my face. "You did this. *You*, Drake." I shove a finger into his chest.

He grabs my wrist and pushes it away. "No," he says, teeth clenched. "What I did was change my life around for you. What I did was give up the best fucking job *for you*."

My heart stops, along with everything else around me. My phone rings in my hand, but it goes largely unnoticed.

"What are you talking about? What did you give up?"

Dropping his chin to his chest, Drake takes a deep breath. When he looks up, his eyes are glossy. "Everything."

I swear I hear him murmur, *including my heart*, but I can't be sure because he pushes past me and reaches for the door.

"Oh no, you don't get to tell me you gave up everything and then just leave," I say, grabbing his arm. I dig my heels into the floor to keep him from walking away.

"Why not? You were going to walk away from me."

"You said—"

"I know what I said, Abigail. I know what you heard. But what you didn't hear was me stepping down from my position as chief surgeon into a staff surgeon role. When I said we wouldn't date while I was in a position of authority over you, I meant it literally. I gave up that part of my job so we could be together without breaking their stupid policy. And they agreed not only to keep you on until your contract expires, but longer, if you wanted."

I stand still, unable to find words. I thought he had given up on us…on me. All of the shattered pieces of my heart somehow snap back in place. Every doubt melts away as though it was never there.

My heart starts beating again, only this time it's stronger. This time, it slams against my ribs so hard I'd swear the stupid thing was trying to throw itself at Drake. But with the pained look on his face—a look I caused—I'm not sure he'd want it.

"I'm sorry." I take a tentative step forward, but Drake holds up his hand, stopping me. "I didn't know. You should've told me. You should've let me sit in on that meeting."

"I should've done a lot of things differently." His tone is cold and emotionless. "The first being thinking long and hard about giving up so much for someone like you."

His words are a slap to the face. "What's that supposed to mean?"

"You're being a coward, Abigail. You say you're leaving because of what I said, but I think you're using that as an excuse. I think you're too scared to stay. You'd rather have safe and comfortable than something scary and new, and I gave you the excuse you needed—handed it over on a silver fucking platter."

I can't believe he thinks that. Pinching my lips together, I shake my head. "That's not true. I was ready to move here, to change all of my plans to be with you."

"Then why were you trying to bail at the first sign of trouble? Trouble that didn't even really exist if you would've taken the time to talk to me. God, Abigail," he growls. "I was excited to come over here and tell you what I'd done. I figured you'd be just as thrilled. We would celebrate, make love, and then I'd take it a step further and ask you to move in with me. And now everything is fucked up, and my position is gone."

"I didn't ask you to give that up. I never would've asked you to give up your job for me!"

"I know you didn't. But I wanted to, Abigail. That's how much I care for you, that's how much I want to see where this thing between us could go. That's also why I didn't want you in there. I knew you would've thrown a fit if you knew what I was about to do."

I hate this. I hate that he did something so amazing for me and we're fighting over it. Mostly, I hate that I was about to walk away. He's right; I am a coward.

"I'm sorry, Drake. You're right. I should've talked to you first."

Slowly, the insecurities start to creep back in, wrapping themselves around my brain and my heart.

Maybe he's right. Maybe this was my way of getting out. I thought I was ready for such a big change, but what if this was my subconscious telling me I'm not?

"Now what?" he asks. "Are you going back to Texas? Is that what you want?"

"I don't know." I raise my arms and drop them. "I don't know what I want," I say, trying to make sense of the thoughts racing in my head. "I need a minute to process everything and think about it."

"What is there to think about?" he asks desperately. "You either want to be with me or you don't. Which is it?"

"It isn't that easy."

"It is," he shouts. "It *is* that easy."

"Not for me," I yell back, hating the sound of my voice. Huffing out a breath, I take a step back. "It's not that easy for me. I need some time to think about what I want."

"Take all the time you need."

Drake doesn't look at me as he walks out of my apartment…and my life.

The door slams shut.

I sit down and rest my head in my hands, squeezing my eyes shut tight.

God, he's so infuriating.

And sexy and sweet and kind and thoughtful.

I'm an idiot.

Holy shit, what have I done? The first little spark of anxiety, and I let it control me. I allow it to cause doubt. And maybe a small piece of me wanted to hurt him the way his words hurt me. But now I feel like shit because Drake's gone, and he thinks I don't want to be with him. He thinks I have second thoughts, when really I don't.

I want Drake Merritt more than I've ever wanted anything or anyone.

Grabbing my purse, I race out of my apartment, but his car is already gone. I watch his taillights as he turns right at the end of my road and disappears from sight.

Chapter 14

Drake

I pull into my garage, throw the Tahoe in park, and stare sightlessly at the stethoscope sitting in my passenger seat, wishing I'd waited to step down as chief. I made it through medical school *and* my residency without letting a woman cloud my judgment. And then Abigail walked into my life.

Fuck.

It's only been ten minutes, and I already miss her. How had he become such a big part of me in such a short amount of time? And how in the hell am I supposed to forget about her? Before Hannah's wedding, I was certain I'd never find a woman to hold my attention. And then Abigail caught my eye. One taste and I was hooked. She ruined me for every other woman because she's so goddamn perfect. Now nothing less than her will ever do.

The sound of a car door slamming shut snaps me out my funk.

"Please, Lord, don't let my neighbors throw another party tonight," I mutter.

My patience is wearing thin. I'm exhausted, irritated, and a little heartbroken. If they start blaring their music again, I just might snap.

I grab my stethoscope and drape it around my neck, then slide out of my car. Rather than going in through the garage, I head to the front so I can grab my mail.

"I lied."

I stop mid-step at the sound of Abigail's voice, but I don't turn around. I can't look at her or I'll cave, and she needs to try a little harder.

"I want you, Drake Merritt. I don't need to think about it."

I take a deep breath, gathering all of the strength and willpower I have. "Go home, Abigail." I proceed to the front porch, where I open my mailbox and pull out a stack of mail.

"No. You might be ready to give up, but I'm not. If you're not ready to fight for us, that's okay. I've got enough strength for both of us, and you're not going to walk away from me."

I hear her shoes crunch against what's left of the snow, and this time when she speaks, her voice is much closer.

"You asked me if I was going back to Texas, and the answer is no. And I don't need time to think about it or process things. I just need you, Drake."

"Abigail…" I stick my key in the lock and push open the front door. "I can't do this with you right now."

"You were right. I'm a coward," she says. Her voice is shaky and desperate, and it pulls at something inside of me.

I turn around.

"I'm uptight, and I'm a coward, but I'm also determined." Tears fill her eyes, and she takes a hesitant step forward. "And I'm going to fight for you, Drake. I'm going to fight for you, and then I'm going to move in with you like you wanted, and then I'm going to organize the hell out of your kitchen…" She takes a shuddery breath before continuing. "And laundry room and bathroom and probably your bedroom too."

Her words cause the tiniest crack in the armor I've put up around my heart. And I think she can see it, because she takes another step forward. "I'll set two alarms every night so we both get up on time, and I'll check those alarms a million times until I get settled in."

Fuck, that's what I want. That's what I've always wanted.

"Abigail—"

"I'll check the refrigerator at least twice every time I shut it."

This time, I take a step toward Abigail, and her eyes widen.

"I like it when you check the refrigerator," I tell her. "I think it's cute."

Her smile almost brings me to my knees.

"I'll touch the outlet every time I unplug something, no matter what it is."

"I'm okay with that."

"Sometimes when I get nervous, I count my steps, or tiles on the ceiling, or cracks in the floor—whatever I can find. It'll get annoying."

"Numbers are my thing."

She tilts her head. "I thought biology was your thing?"

"Biology, numbers, and you. You're my thing."

"I'm highly imperfect."

"Perfect is overrated."

"People will laugh at me, and they'll laugh at you for being with me."

"Let them laugh." I grab Abigail's wrist and tug her forward. She collapses against my body. She's warm and soft and feels perfect in my arms.

I'm never letting her go again.

"I'm so sorry, Drake. I'm sorry I tried to leave without talking to you. I'm sorry for not telling you sooner that I'm head-over-heels in love with you, and I'm sorry for—"

"What did you just say?"

"I'm sorry for not talking to you?" she asks.

"No, after that."

"Oh." She nods dramatically and wraps her arms around my neck. Her sweet lips press against my jaw and slowly work their way up until they're resting against my ear. My body shudders. "I'm head-over-heels in love with you," she whispers.

She squeals when I scoop her into my arms. "I love you too, Abigail Darwin."

"You do?"

I carry her over the threshold, kick the door shut, and sit down on the couch. I settle her on my lap.

"Very much so. I love how expressive your eyes are. I love your smile and your belly laugh. I love the way you chew on your lip when you're concentrating. I love how honest and open you've been with me. And I really love your quirks."

She blushes. "They're silly."

"I prefer *endearing*."

"Endearing is good. I like that word."

"But mostly, I just love you. I love you more than I've ever loved another human being."

"Be sure, Drake, because my quirks may be endearing right now, but I promise you they're going to get irritating. I've grown to hate them, and I know you will too."

"We'll work through them together, but trust me, Abigail; there is absolutely nothing I could ever hate about you."

Chapter 15

Abby

How did I get so lucky? Drake's warm hands run the length of my back and settle on my hips. His grip tightens, and the urge to kiss him is strong. I lean in a few inches until our mouths meet. His lips are warm and sweet, and his familiar scent surrounds me. It's the smell of stability and love... It's the smell of home.

A rush of emotion clogs my throat. I push up onto my knees, hovering over him so I can deepen the kiss. My tongue traces the seam of his mouth, and he opens with a groan. He runs his tongue along my bottom lip and sucks gently, sending a shiver of need through my body. My nipples stiffen. I plunge my fingers into his hair, wanting and needing so much more.

He breaks the kiss and rests his forehead against my shoulder. "I want you so bad," he pants. "But don't you think we should talk about what happened first?"

"I can barely think with your hands on me, let alone talk."

"Okay." He nods. "We'll talk later."

Next thing I know he's switched our positions, and now he's above me on the couch. His big body pushes me against the cushions. He trails kisses along my jaw, down my neck, and runs the length of my collarbone.

He slips a hand under my shirt, slowing dragging it up my body. I lift up enough for him to tug it off, and I don't even care where it ends up because Drake's warm breath against my breast is all I can concentrate on. My nipples are tight, straining against my bra, begging for his mouth. Drake puts a finger in the top of the cup and pulls it down. My breast falls into his waiting mouth. I jerk forward when he closes his lips over the tight bud. There's a flood of moisture between my legs, and I grind my hips against his, needing the friction.

Damn, he's so big.

"Fuck," he breathes.

Our moans of pleasure and harsh breathing fill the room. It's the sexiest sound I've ever heard. Drake's hand slides down the back of my thigh. Hooking his fingers beneath my knee, he hoists my leg around his waist and cups my ass. Awareness slides through me at his confident touch. I untangle my hands from his hair, grip the back of his shirt, and pull it off. My fingers trace a path down his back, and then I slide them over his six-pack. I dip them into the front of his scrub pants and find his cock hard. My legs quiver as I find a bead of pre-cum gathered at the tip. I wrap my fingers around his long, thick shaft.

"Fuck yeah," he moans, thrusting into my hips.

Heat bubbles low in my belly. The ache for more urges me to pulse my hips in rhythm with his. I stroke him from base to tip as we grind against each other. But it isn't enough.

"I need more. Please, Drake. I need you to fuck me."

* * * *

Drake

This woman is going to be the death of me. If the lush scent of her body wasn't enough to turn me on, her soft little moans would definitely tip me over the edge. My blood is pumping with need, but even though she's begging me to fuck her, I can't. Not yet at least.

I reach for Abigail's pants. She lifts her hips, and I yank them off, along with her panties. My beautiful angel is laid out before me.

"Drake…" Abigail's whispered pleas spur me on, and I shoulder my way between her thighs. Curling my arms around her knees, I spread her apart while pulling her toward me. Her clit is swollen, and when I circle it with my tongue, she cries out in pleasure.

"Oh, God, Drake. Please…" Her words fade into a whimper, causing my cock to jerk.

I run my tongue up her slit. When I cover her clit with my lips and suck rhythmically, Abigail's legs begin to tremble. Her knees fall open, and I accept the invitation by sliding two fingers deep into her body.

My fingers pump in rhythm with my tongue. I work her slowly at first and then speed up—licking, sucking, and tasting my sweet girl. I push her until she's writhing beneath me, and it doesn't take long until she loses control.

Her hands grip the back of my head, locking into my hair as she pushes my face against her core. Her body convulses, thighs tightening around my head as she bathes my tongue in her sweet, warm scent.

If I don't get inside of her in the next thirty seconds, I'm going to explode. When her legs relax, I sit up, and we both work frantically to get my pants and boxers off. Her body is still trembling when I cover it with my own.

A rush of air pushes from her lungs when I slide inside her with one deep thrust. Tight—she's so tight my vision blurs, but I don't stop. She's every fantasy come to life, and she's mine. The need to claim her, mark her as mine, grows with each thrust until I find myself pumping harder and deeper. She accepts everything I give her.

"Harder," she begs, her head dropping back onto the couch. She raises her hips, leaving them in the air, and the shift allows me farther into her body. I want to slow down a few notches, milk this moment for all it is, but I'm too far gone.

Abigail's body squirms against mine, wild and frantic, chasing something only I can provide. She does something that causes her muscles to tighten around me.

"Oh, fuck," I tell her. "Do that again."

She continues to contract her muscles, each time sucking me in. A tingle of awareness starts low in my spine, working its way up. A gentle pressure unfolding causes warmth to radiate throughout my body. Abigail claws at my back, chasing her release while my own builds to the point of explosion.

"Don't stop," she moans, rocking her hips.

I pull back and plunge forward, over and over again.

Her body tenses beneath mine, and then there's a flood of moisture. "Oh, Drake. Oh, God, yes. Just like that. Keep going." Her hips buck as she rides out her bliss.

Triumph pumps through me, sending me hurtling over the edge. I bury my face in the crook of her neck as waves of pleasure crash over me.

By the time her body stops shuddering, I'm too exhausted to move. We stay like this for several long seconds, and then I push up onto my elbows. Abigail looks sated, her eyes hooded. She's wearing a crooked smile.

"So, that was make-up sex?" she asks, running her fingers through my hair.

"I guess so."

Her eyes drift shut. "Remind me to pick fights with you more often."

"I don't like it when we fight," I admit.

Her eyes open. She cradles my cheek in her hand and draws me in for a kiss. "I don't either. I really am sorry for overreacting today. I promise I won't do it again."

"I'm sorry too. Next time I'll talk to you before I make any big decisions."

"See?" she says proudly. "We're good at this relationship stuff."

"And we're only going to get better. Are you really moving in with me?"

"If you're sure you're ready for my brand of crazy."

"I was born ready."

Epilogue

Two years later

Abby

"Come on, baby," Drake pants.

I'm convinced he's part animal. The man just doesn't stop. He has more stamina than what I believe is humanly possible, and he's used that stamina to push my body further than it's ever gone. And it feels so damn good it hurts. My legs are a quivering mass of Jell-O, and I'm not sure how much longer I'm going to last.

"Oh, God," I moan.

"Come on, Abigail. Almost there, baby."

"I think you said that to me last night in bed." I plow forward even though I want nothing more than to give up. Drake's ass bounces in front of me, and it's the only thing keeping me going.

"I'll say it to you again tonight if you get your tight little ass to the top of this hill."

"There better be some warm brownies or freshly baked chocolate chip cookies up there, or I'm never hiking with you again."

"There aren't any baked goods, but I promise you'll love what I have planned."

"I better," I huff. "Because my lungs are on fire."

I see Drake stop up ahead, so I dig in and then nearly collapse beside him. Hands on my knees, I hunch forward to try to catch my breath. It pisses me off that he's standing with his hands on his hips, staring at God knows what, and he's not even breaking a sweat.

His warm hand lands on my back, and I shake it off. "You're not human."

"Come on, it wasn't that bad."

"You're right. It was worse."

Drake laughs. "Stand up."

"I'm not sure I can."

With a hand to my arm and another on my back, he helps me to standing, and I nearly lose my breath again.

"Oh my..." I look out over the most spectacular view of the snowcapped mountains. A lake below glistens in the afternoon sun. "This is heaven on Earth."

"I think so too." His fingers link with mine. "But I didn't bring you up here for the view."

"You didn't?" I look up at him.

"Nope." He removes his backpack and reaches inside, pulling out a rolled-up paper. "Remember when we promised to talk through any big decisions?"

"Yes."

"And do you remember when we were at the diner, talking about our dreams?" I nod, and he continues. "At the time I couldn't really think of one. But that's changed."

He hands me the paper. I drop my backpack to the ground and slowly unroll it, careful not to tear it.

"What is this?" I ask, trying to make sense of all the lines. "I mean, I know they're plans of some sort. Are they house plans?"

Drake looks at the paper and curses. "Shit. Wrong paper."

He pulls another paper from his bag, unrolls it, and holds it open for me to see. "It's our dreams."

My eyes scan the drawing of a large building before landing on the words at the bottom: Cunningham Falls Surgery Center and Turtle Sanctuary.

"Oh my God, Drake." Tears fill my eyes as I look at him. "What is this?"

"Our dream, if you're willing to build it with me. When I was in medical school, I interned for a doctor who owned his own surgical center. He used it as a means to provide more affordable healthcare to his small community, and I think Cunningham Falls and the surrounding areas would benefit from having something similar. We can provide medical care at more affordable rates to patients who would otherwise go without."

"We? I know nothing about running a surgical center."

"And I know nothing about owning a turtle sanctuary."

I smile. "You're not serious about opening a turtle sanctuary."

"Why not? It's your dream."

"Does Montana even have turtles? I don't think I've seen one turtle since I've been here."

"I don't know, but I'll make it my mission to find them. I'll drive all over the country adopting them from animal shelters, if I have to."

Damn, he's good. "You'd do that for me?"

"Abigail…" Drake curls a hand around the back of my neck. "Haven't you figured it out yet? I'd do anything for you. And I want to build our dream together. We'll take it slow. I've done a ton of research already, and if you're in, we can start building this spring."

"Of course I'm in," I say, throwing myself into his arms.

Drake catches me and spins me around. "That's a yes?"

"Yes! Let's do it." I pull back and look at him. "But you didn't have to bring me all the way up here to ask me about this."

"Oh, that's not why I brought you up here," he says, dipping his hand into his pocket.

"It's not?"

Drake shakes his head and drops to one knee, and everything around me comes to a screeching halt.

"Oh my."

Taking my left hand in his, Drake smiles up at me. "Abigail Darwin, you have been the brightest light in my life. You give me strength and courage to chase my dreams and be the best man I can be. You make me laugh and smile, and even though your quirks are getting a little annoying like you promised, I can't imagine living my life without them. I can't imagine living my life without you. You've taught me that love doesn't have to perfect; it just has to be real, and I want to spend the rest of my life loving you."

He slips a gorgeous, emerald-cut diamond on my ring finger. "Will you marry me?"

"Yes." I drop to my knees and wipe tears from my cheeks.

Drake holds my face in his big, strong hands and kisses me long and deep. We kiss for minutes, or maybe it's hours. I really don't know because when I'm in Drake's arms, the whole world seems to fade away.

He's right; our love isn't perfect. Neither is our life or either one of us. But Drake has taught me that sometimes the most imperfect things can be pretty damn perfect. And I wouldn't have it any other way.

Sign up for the 1001 Dark Nights Newsletter
and be entered to win a Tiffany Lock necklace.

There's a contest every quarter!

Go to www.1001DarkNights.com to subscribe.

As a bonus, all subscribers can download
FIVE FREE exclusive books!

Discover the Kristen Proby Crossover Collection

Soaring with Fallon: A Big Sky Novel
By Kristen Proby

Fallon McCarthy has climbed the corporate ladder. She's had the office with the view, the staff, and the plaque on her door. The unexpected loss of her grandmother taught her that there's more to life than meetings and conference calls, so she quit, and is happy to be a nomad, checking off items on her bucket list as she takes jobs teaching yoga in each place she lands in. She's happy being free, and has no interest in being tied down.

When Noah King gets the call that an eagle has been injured, he's not expecting to find a beautiful stranger standing vigil when he arrives. Rehabilitating birds of prey is Noah's passion, it's what he lives for, and he doesn't have time for a nosy woman who's suddenly taken an interest in Spread Your Wings sanctuary.

But Fallon's gentle nature, and the way she makes him laugh, and *feel* again draws him in. When it comes time for Fallon to move on, will Noah's love be enough for her to stay, or will he have to find the strength to let her fly?

* * * *

Wicked Force: A Wicked Horse Vegas/Big Sky Novella
By Sawyer Bennett

From *New York Times* and *USA Today* bestselling author Sawyer Bennett…

Joslyn Meyers has taken the celebrity world by storm, drawing the attention of millions. But one fan's affections has gone too far, and she's running to the one place she hopes he'll never find her – back home to Cunningham Falls.

Kynan McGrath leads The Jameson Group, a world-class security organization, and he's ready to do what it takes to keep Joslyn safe, even if it means giving up his own life in return. The one thing he's not prepared to lose, though, is his heart.

* * * *

Crazy Imperfect Love: A Dirty Dicks/Big Sky Novella
By KL Grayson

From *USA Today* bestselling author KL Grayson…

Abigail Darwin needs one thing in life: consistency. Okay, make that two things: consistency and order. Tired of being shackled to her obsessive-compulsive mind, Abigail is determined to break free. Which is why she's shaking things up.

Fresh out of nursing school, she takes a traveling nurse position. A new job in a new city every few months? That's a sure-fire way to keep her from settling down and falling into old habits. First stop, Cunningham Falls, Montana.

The only problem? She didn't plan on falling in love with the quaint little town, and she sure as heck didn't plan on falling for its resident surgeon, Dr. Drake Merritt

Laid back, messy, and spontaneous, Drake is everything she's not. But he is completely smitten by the new, quirky nurse working on the med-surg floor of the hospital.

Abby puts up a good fight, but Drake is determined to break through her carefully erected walls to find out what makes her tick. And sigh and moan and smile and laugh. Because he really loves her laugh.

But falling in love isn't part of Abby's plan. Will Drake have what it takes to convince her that the best things in life come from doing what scares us the most?

* * * *

Worth Fighting For: A Warrior Fight Club/Big Sky Novella
By Laura Kaye

From *New York Times* and *USA Today* bestselling author Laura Kaye…

Getting in deep has never felt this good…

Commercial diving instructor Tara Hunter nearly lost everything in an accident that saw her medically discharged from the navy. With the help of the Warrior Fight Club, she's fought hard to overcome her fears and get back in the water where she's always felt most at home. At work, she's tough, serious, and doesn't tolerate distractions. Which is why finding her gorgeous one-night stand on her new dive team is such a problem.

Former navy deep-sea diver Jesse Anderson just can't seem to stop making mistakes—the latest being the hot-as-hell night he'd spent with his new partner. This job is his second chance, and Jesse knows he shouldn't mix business with pleasure. But spending every day with Tara's smart mouth and sexy curves makes her so damn hard to resist.

Joining a wounded warrior MMA training program seems like the perfect way to blow off steam—until Jesse finds that Tara belongs too. Now they're getting in deep and taking each other down day and night, and even though it breaks all the rules, their inescapable attraction might just be the only thing truly worth fighting for.

* * * *

Nothing Without You: A Forever Yours/Big Sky Novella
By Monica Murphy

From *New York Times* and *USA Today* bestselling author Monica Murphy…

Designing wedding cakes is Maisey Henderson's passion. She puts her heart and soul into every cake she makes, especially since she's such a believer in true love. But then Tucker McCloud rolls back into town, reminding her that love is a complete joke. The pro football player is the hottest thing to come out of Cunningham Falls—and the boy who broke Maisey's heart back in high school.

He claims he wants another chance. She says absolutely not. But Maisey's refusal is the ultimate challenge to Tucker. Life is a game, and Tucker's playing to win Maisey's heart—forever.

* * * *

All Stars Fall: A Seaside Pictures/Big Sky Novella
By Rachel Van Dyken

From *New York Times* and *USA Today* bestselling author Rachel Van Dyken…

She *left.*
Two words I can't really get out of my head.
She left *us.*
Three more words that make it that much worse.
Three being another word I can't seem to wrap my mind around.
Three kids under the age of six, and she left because she missed it. Because her dream had never been to have a family, no her dream had been to marry a rockstar and live the high life.

Moving my recording studio to Seaside Oregon seems like the best idea in the world right now especially since Seaside Oregon has turned into the place for celebrities to stay and raise families in between touring and producing. It would be lucrative to make the move, but I'm doing it for my kids because they need normal, they deserve normal. And me? Well, I just need a break and help, that too. I need a sitter and fast. Someone who won't flip me off when I ask them to sign an Iron Clad NDA, someone who won't sell our pictures to the press, and most of all? Someone who looks absolutely nothing like my ex-wife.

He's tall.
That was my first instinct when I saw the notorious Trevor Wood, drummer for the rock band Adrenaline, in the local coffee shop. He ordered a tall black coffee which made me smirk, and five minutes later I somehow agreed to interview for a nanny position. I couldn't help it; the smaller one had gum stuck in her hair while the eldest was standing on his feet and asking where babies came from. He looked so pathetic, so damn sexy and pathetic that rather than be star-struck, I took pity. I knew though; I knew the minute I signed that NDA, the minute our fingers brushed and my body became insanely aware of how close he was—I was in dangerous territory, I just didn't know how dangerous until it was too late. Until I fell for the star and realized that no matter how high they are in the sky—they're still human and fall just as hard.

* * * *

Hold On: A Play On/Big Sky Novella
By Samantha Young

From *New York Times* and *USA Today* bestselling author Samantha Young...

Autumn O'Dea has always tried to see the best in people while her big brother, Killian, has always tried to protect her from the worst. While their lonely upbringing made Killian a cynic, it isn't in Autumn's nature to be anything but warm and open. However, after a series of relationship disasters and the unsettling realization that she's drifting aimlessly through life, Autumn wonders if she's left herself too vulnerable to the world. Deciding some distance from the security blanket of her brother and an unmotivated life in Glasgow is exactly what she needs to find herself, Autumn takes up her friend's offer to stay at a ski resort in the snowy hills of Montana. Some guy-free alone time on Whitetail Mountain sounds just the thing to get to know herself better.

However, she wasn't counting on colliding into sexy Grayson King on the slopes. Autumn has never met anyone like Gray. Confident, smart, with a wicked sense of humor, he makes the men she dated seem like boys. Her attraction to him immediately puts her on the defense because being open-hearted in the past has only gotten it broken. Yet it becomes increasingly difficult to resist a man who is not only determined to seduce her, but adamant about helping her find her purpose in life and embrace the person she is. Autumn knows she shouldn't fall for Gray. It can only end badly. After all their lives are divided by an ocean and their inevitable separation is just another heart break away...

Discover 1001 Dark Nights Collection Six

DRAGON CLAIMED by Donna Grant
A Dark Kings Novella

ASHES TO INK by Carrie Ann Ryan
A Montgomery Ink: Colorado Springs Novella

ENSNARED by Elisabeth Naughton
An Eternal Guardians Novella

EVERMORE by Corinne Michaels
A Salvation Series Novella

VENGEANCE by Rebecca Zanetti
A Dark Protectors/Rebels Novella

ELI'S TRIUMPH by Joanna Wylde
A Reapers MC Novella

CIPHER by Larissa Ione
A Demonica Underworld Novella

RESCUING MACIE by Susan Stoker
A Delta Force Heroes Novella

ENCHANTED by Lexi Blake
A Masters and Mercenaries Novella

TAKE THE BRIDE by Carly Phillips
A Knight Brothers Novella

INDULGE ME by J. Kenner
A Stark Ever After Novella

THE KING by Jennifer L. Armentrout
A Wicked Novella

QUIET MAN by Kristen Ashley
A Dream Man Novella

ABANDON by Rachel Van Dyken
A Seaside Pictures Novella

THE OPEN DOOR by Laurelin Paige
A Found Duet Novella

CLOSER by Kylie Scott
A Stage Dive Novella

SOMETHING JUST LIKE THIS by Jennifer Probst
A Stay Novella

BLOOD NIGHT by Heather Graham
A Krewe of Hunters Novella

TWIST OF FATE by Jill Shalvis
A Heartbreaker Bay Novella

MORE THAN PLEASURE YOU by Shayla Black
A More Than Words Novella

WONDER WITH ME by Kristen Proby
A With Me In Seattle Novella

THE DARKEST ASSASSIN by Gena Showalter
A Lords of the Underworld Novella

Also from 1001 Dark Nights:
DAMIEN by J. Kenner
A Stark Novel

Discover the World of 1001 Dark Nights

Collection One

Collection Two

Collection Three

Collection Four

Collection Five

Bundles

Discovery Authors

Blue Box Specials

Rising Storm

Liliana Hart's MacKenzie Family

Lexi Blake's Crossover Collection

Kristen Proby's Crossover Collection

About KL Grayson

K.L. Grayson resides in a small town outside of St. Louis, MO. She is entertained daily by her extraordinary husband, who will forever inspire every good quality she writes in a man. Her entire life rests in the palms of six dirty little hands, and when the day is over and those pint-sized cherubs have been washed and tucked into bed, you can find her typing away furiously on her computer. She has a love for alpha-males, brownies, reading, tattoos, sunglasses, and happy endings...and not particularly in that order.

For more information visit http://klgrayson.com/about/

Crazy, Sexy Love
By KL Grayson
Now Available

Three-time world champion bull rider Rhett Allen has never been afraid to get his hands dirty. Hard work, sweat, and determination have gotten him where he is today—and that's holed up in a hospital room, wondering how he let that damn bull buck him off. He's also wondering why he thought it was a good idea to let his twin brother talk him into returning home to heal.

Rhett has a million reasons to come home to Heaven, Texas, and only one reason to stay away. That reason comes in the form of a sweet and feisty girl who stole his heart long before he ever thought to give it away. The only problem…that girl has turned into a stunning woman.

Monroe Gallagher is downright sexy with more curves than County Line Rd. It's been six years since he's seen her, six years since he's felt any form of peace, and six years since she gripped his heart in her delicate little hands and squeezed the life out of it. The longer he's in Heaven, the more he starts to realize that the heart she took from him— the one she crushed into a million pieces—she also never gave back.

* * * *

Chapter 1
Rhett
"Are you crazy?"
The door flies open, hitting the wall behind it with a loud thud, and every man in the locker room—myself included—looks up. My manager, Nikki Atwood, is a sight to behold: big tits, plump ass, and thighs made to squeeze a man's head. And tonight she is dressed to the nines. Any other woman in that outfit would look out of place in a room full of bull riders, but she makes it work. I know every man in here is wondering what it would be like to dirty her prissy little ass up a bit.
Except me.
Been there. Done that.
It's not something I'm proud of, but I was young and dumb, and I

refuse to dwell on mistakes of the past. And in my defense, when I slept with her, she wasn't my manager. Not yet anyway, and I was nursing a broken heart. Had I known she would eventually slide into the role that had belonged to her father, I would've thought twice before getting my dick wet. But that doesn't mean my decision to fuck her would've changed—because I was hurting, and she's hot as hell, and any man would have a hard time turning her down—but maybe I would've given it more thought.

"I ride bulls for a living, darlin'," I tell her. "I'd say crazy is part of the job description."

"Don't get cute with me, Rhett. You know damn well what I'm talking about. A bonus ride? On Lucifer no less."

"I just walked out of that arena with a 92.2 score. Thought you'd be happier about that."

"Oh, I am happy about that, and so are your sponsors." She crosses her arms. "But imagine my surprise when I find out you signed up for a bonus ride. What were you thinking, and why didn't you tell me?"

"I was thinking I could use the extra cash, and if I told you, you'd try to talk me out of it."

Her brow creases, and for a split second I swear I see steam coming out of her ears.

"You're damn right I would've talked you out of it." Nikki stalks toward the middle of the room, plants her hands on her hips, and lifts an eyebrow at some of the other guys, a silent request that they get out.

Lincoln Bennett, my best friend in this business, is the first one to move. Pushing up from the floor, he shoots me a *good luck* look and taps some of the other guys on the shoulder. "Come on. Let's give Rhett some privacy." On his way out of the locker room, he tips his hat to Nikki. "Nicole."

"Thank you, Linc," she says.

She waits for the locker room to clear and then turns to me, eyebrows raised.

She's not going to intimidate me. "What?"

"Don't play dumb. You may be crazy, but no one ever called you dumb."

"I don't know what you want from me." I shrug. "They offered a fifty-grand bonus if I stay on for eight seconds. I couldn't pass that up."

"They offered you fifty grand because no one has been able to stay on that damn bull for longer than four seconds."

"Until me." I shoot her a cocky smile, and she rolls her eyes.

"Until you. Riiiiiiiight," she says. "Lucifer has been responsible for forty-seven injuries this year alone, and unless you've forgotten, you've got commitments outside of the arena, commitments that will earn you well over fifty grand."

"I'm well aware of the risk, and as far as Wrangler and Powerade are con—"

"Gatorade."

"Whatever. The point is, bull riding is my job, and it comes first."

Fifty grand is nothing to Nikki. She was born into money, and even though she works her ass off, she doesn't really need her job.

She may come from cash, but I come from a ranch in Heaven, Texas. My parents—although they're doing well now—have practically killed themselves for every dime they have, and even though I've got a decent cushion in my bank account, it's not enough. It might never be enough. Being a bull rider is a precarious job, and it doesn't always pay the best, which is why I've let her talk me in to a few modeling gigs and the occasional commercial.

Every time I get on one of those bulls, I'm putting my career and my life at risk. If something happens and I lose the ability to work, I need to know I'm going to be financially stable until I find something else to do. So, yes, whether she understands it or not, I need that fifty grand.

"Call it off."

She's smoking crack. "No way."

As Nikki well knows, I don't back down. If I say I'm going to do something, I do it, which is probably why she pinches her lips into a thin line and strides across the room. Her hand hits the door knob and she stops, but doesn't look back.

"You better stay on that bull, Rhett Allen, or so help me God, your ass is mine."

"Not a problem, darlin'."

On behalf of 1001 Dark Nights,

Liz Berry and M.J. Rose would like to thank ~

Steve Berry
Doug Scofield
Kim Guidroz
Jillian Stein
InkSlinger PR
Dan Slater
Asha Hossain
Chris Graham
Fedora Chen
Kasi Alexander
Jessica Johns
Dylan Stockton
Richard Blake
and Simon Lipskar

CPSIA information can be obtained
at www.ICGtesting.com
Printed in the USA
LVHW041817140319
610673LV00002B/198